GREGOR THE
OVERLANDER

THE UNDERLAND CHRONICLES 1
SUZANNE COLLINS

■SCHOLASTIC

Scholastic Children's Books
An imprint of Scholastic Ltd
Euston House, 24 Eversholt Street
London, NW1 1DB, UK
Registered office: Westfield Road, Southam, Warwickshire, CV47 0RA
SCHOLASTIC and associated logos are trademarks and/or registered
trademarks of Scholastic Inc.

First published in the US by Scholastic Inc., 2003
This edition published in the UK by Scholastic Ltd., 2013

Text © Suzanne Collins, 2003

The right of Suzanne Collins to be identified as the author
of this work has been asserted by her.

ISBN 978 1407 13703 2

A CIP catalogue record for this book
is available from the British Library.

Printed and bound by CPI Group (UK) Ltd, Croydon, CR0 4YY

Papers used by Scholastic Children's Books are made
from wood grown in sustainable forests.

1 3 5 7 9 10 8 6 4 2

This is a work of fiction. Names, characters, places, incidents and dialogues are
products of the author's imagination or are used fictitiously. Any resemblance to
actual people, living or dead, events of locals is entirely coincidental.

www.scholastic.co.uk/zone

ALSO BY SUZANNE COLLINS

GREGOR THE
OVERLANDER

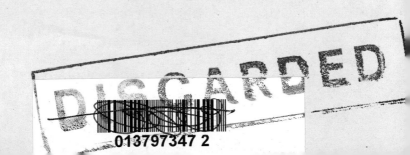

ALSO BY SUZANNE COLLINS:

The Underland Chronicles:
Gregor the Overlander
Gregor and the Prophecy of Bane
Gregor and the Curse of the Warmbloods
Gregor and the Marks of Secret
Gregor and the Code of Claw

The Hunger Games Trilogy:
The Hunger Games
Catching Fire
Mockingjay

FOR MY MOM AND DAD

PART I

THE FALL

CHAPTER

1

Gregor had pressed his forehead against the screen for so long, he could feel a pattern of tiny checks above his eyebrows. He ran his fingers over the bumps and resisted the impulse to let out a primal caveman scream. It was building up in his chest, that long gutteral howl reserved for real emergencies — like when you ran into a saber-toothed tiger without your club, or your fire went out during the Ice Age. He even went so far as to open his mouth and take a deep breath before he banged his head back into the screen with a quiet sound of frustration. "Ergh."

What was the point, anyway? It wouldn't change one thing. Not the heat, not the boredom, not the endless space of summer laid out before him.

He considered waking up Boots, his two-year-old sister,

just for a little distraction, but he let her sleep. At least she was cool in the air-conditioned bedroom she shared with their seven-year-old sister, Lizzie, and their grandma. It was the only air-conditioned room in the apartment. On really hot nights, Gregor and his mother could spread quilts on the floor to sleep, but with five in the room it wasn't cool, just lukewarm.

Gregor got an ice cube from the freezer and rubbed it on his face. He stared out at the courtyard where a stray dog sniffed around an overflowing trash can. The dog set its paws on the rim, tipping the can and sending the garbage across the sidewalk. Gregor caught a glimpse of a couple of shadowy shapes scurrying along the wall and grimaced. Rats. He never really got used to them.

Otherwise, the courtyard was deserted. Usually it was full of kids playing ball, jumping rope, or swinging around the creaky jungle gym. But this morning, the bus had left for camp, and every kid between the ages of four and fourteen had been on it. Except one.

"I'm sorry, baby, you can't go," his mother had told him a few weeks ago. And she really had been sorry, too, he could tell by the look on her face. "Someone has to watch Boots while I'm at work, and we both know your grandma can't handle it anymore."

Of course he knew it. For the last year his grandma had been slipping in and out of reality. One minute she was clear as a bell and the next she was calling him Simon. Who was Simon? He had no idea.

It would have been different a few years ago. His mom

only worked part-time then, and his dad, who'd taught high school science, was off summers. He'd have taken care of Boots. But since his dad disappeared one night, Gregor's role in the family had changed. He was the oldest, so he'd picked up a lot of the slack. Looking after his little sisters was a big part of it.

So all Gregor had said was, "That's okay, Mom. Camp's for kids, anyway." He'd shrugged to show that, at eleven, he was past caring about things like camp. But somehow that had made her look sadder.

"Do you want Lizzie to stay home with you? Give you some company?" she'd asked.

A look of panic had crossed Lizzie's face at this suggestion. She probably would have burst into tears if Gregor hadn't refused the offer. "Nah, let her go. I'll be fine with Boots."

So, here he was. Not fine. Not fine spending the whole summer cooped up with a two-year-old and his grandma who thought he was someone named —

"Simon!" he heard his grandma call from the bedroom. Gregor shook his head but he couldn't help smiling a little.

"Coming, Grandma!" he called back, and crunched down the rest of his ice cube.

A golden glow filled the room as the afternoon sunlight tried to force its way through the shades. His grandma lay on the bed covered by a thin cotton quilt. Every patch on the quilt had come from a dress she had made for herself through the years. In her more lucid moments, she'd talk to Gregor through the quilt. "This polka-dotted swiss I wore to my cousin Lucy's graduation when I was eleven, this lemon yellow was a Sunday dress, and this white is in actual fact a corner of my wedding dress, I do not lie."

This, however, was not a lucid moment. "Simon," she said, her face showing relief at the sight of him. "I thought you forgot your lunch pail. You'll get hungry plowing."

His grandma had been raised on a farm in Virginia and had come to New York when she married his grandfather. She had never really taken to it. Sometimes Gregor was secretly glad that she could return to that farm in her mind. And a little envious. It wasn't any fun sitting around their apartment all the time. By now the bus would probably be arriving at camp and Lizzie and the rest of the kids would —

"Ge-go!" squealed a little voice. A curly head popped over the side of the crib. "Me out!" Boots stuck the soggy end of a stuffed dog's tail in her mouth and reached up both arms to him. Gregor lifted his sister high in the air and blew a loud raspberry on her stomach. She giggled and the dog fell to the floor. He set her down to retrieve it.

"Take your hat!" said Grandma, still somewhere back in Virginia.

Gregor took her hand to try to focus her attention. "You want a cold drink, Grandma? How about a root beer?"

She laughed. "A root beer? What is it, my birthday?"

How did you answer something like that?

Gregor gave her hand a squeeze and scooped up Boots. "I'll be right back," he said loudly.

His grandma was still laughing to herself. "A root beer!" she said, and wiped her eyes.

In the kitchen, Gregor filled a glass with icy root beer

and made Boots a bottle of milk.

"Code," she beamed, pressing it to her face.

"Yes, nice and cold, Boots," said Gregor.

A knock on the door startled him. The peephole had been useless for a good forty years. He called through the door, "Who is it?"

"It's Mrs. Cormaci, darling. I told your mother I'd sit with your grandma at four!" a voice called back. Then Gregor remembered the pile of laundry he was supposed to do. At least he'd get out of the apartment.

He opened the door to find Mrs. Cormaci looking wilted in the heat. "Hello, you! Isn't it awful? I tell you I do not suffer heat gladly!" She bustled into the apartment patting her face with an old bandanna. "Oh, you dream, is that for me?" she said, and before he could answer she was gulping down the root beer like she'd been lost in the desert.

"Sure," Gregor mumbled, heading back to the kitchen to fix another. He didn't really mind Mrs. Cormaci, and today it was almost a relief to see her. "Great, Day One and I'm looking forward to a trip to the laundry room," Gregor thought. "By September, I'll probably be ecstatic when we get the phone bill."

Mrs. Cormaci held out her glass for a refill. "So, when are you going to let me read your tarot, Mister? You know I've got the gift," she said. Mrs. Cormaci posted signs by the mailboxes offering to read tarot cards for people at ten bucks a shot. "No charge for you," she always told Gregor. He never accepted because he had a sneaking suspicion Mrs. Cormaci would end up asking a lot more questions than he would. Questions he couldn't answer. Questions about his dad.

He mumbled something about the laundry and hurried off to collect it. Knowing Mrs. Cormaci, she probably had a deck of tarot cards right in her pocket.

Down in the laundry room, Gregor sorted clothes as best he could. Whites, darks, colors . . . what was he supposed to do with Boots's black-and-white-striped shorts? He tossed them in the darks feeling sure it was the wrong decision.

Most of their clothes were kind of grayish anyway — from age, not bad laundry choices. All Gregor's shorts were just his winter pants cut off at the knees, and he only had a few T-shirts that fit from last year, but what did it matter if he was going to be locked in the apartment all summer?

"Ball!" cried Boots in distress. "Ball!"

Gregor reached his arm between the dryers and pulled out an old tennis ball Boots had been chasing around. He picked off the dryer lint and tossed it across the room. Boots ran after it like a puppy.

"What a mess," thought Gregor, laughing a little. "What a sticky, crusty, dusty mess!" The remains of her lunch, egg salad and chocolate pudding, were still evident on Boots's face and shirt. She had colored her hands purple with washable markers that Gregor thought maybe a sandblaster could remove, and her diaper sagged down around her knees. It was just too hot to put her into shorts.

Boots ran back to him with the ball, dryer lint floating in her curls. Her sweaty face beamed as she held out the ball. "What makes you so happy, Boots?" he asked.

"Ball!" she said, and then banged her head into his knee, on purpose, to speed him up. Gregor tossed the ball down the alley between the washers and the dryers. Boots flew after it.

As the game continued, Gregor tried to remember the last time he'd felt as happy as Boots did with her ball. He had had some decent times over the past couple of years. The city middle school band had gotten to play at Carnegie Hall. That was pretty cool. He'd even had a short solo on his saxophone. Things were always better when he played music; the notes seemed to carry him to a different world altogether.

Running track was good, too. Pushing his body on and on until everything had been drummed out of his mind.

But if he was honest with himself, Gregor knew it had been years since he'd felt real happiness. "Exactly two years, seven months, and thirteen days," he thought. He didn't try to count, but the numbers automatically tallied up in his head. He had some inner calculator that always knew exactly how long his dad had been gone.

Boots could be happy. She wasn't even born when it happened. Lizzie was only four. But Gregor had been eight and had missed nothing; like the frantic calls to the police, who had acted almost bored with the fact that his dad had vanished into thin air. Clearly they'd thought he'd run off. They'd even implied it was with another woman.

That just wasn't true. If there was anything Gregor knew, it was that his father loved his mother, that he loved him and Lizzie, that he would have loved Boots.

But then — how could he have left them without a word? Gregor couldn't believe his dad would abandon the family and never look back. "Accept it," he whispered to himself. "He's dead." A wave of pain swept through him. It wasn't true. It couldn't be true. His dad was coming back because . . . because . . . because what? Because he wanted it so badly it must be true? Because they needed him? "No," thought Gregor. "It's because I can feel it. I know he's coming back."

The washer spun to a stop, and Gregor piled the clothes into a couple of dryers. "And when he gets back, he'd better have a really good explanation for where he's been!" muttered Gregor as he slammed the dryer door shut. "Like he got bumped on the head and forgot who he was. Or he was kidnapped by aliens." Lots of people got kidnapped by aliens on TV. Maybe it could happen.

He thought about different possibilities a lot in his head, but they rarely mentioned his dad at home. There was an unspoken agreement that his dad would return. All the neighbors thought he'd just taken off. The adults never mentioned it, and neither did most of the kids — about half of them only lived with one parent, anyway. Strangers sometimes asked, though. After about a year of trying to explain it, Gregor came up with the story that his parents were divorced and his dad lived in California. It was a lie but people believed it, while no one seemed to believe the truth. Whatever that was.

"And after he gets home I can take him —," Gregor said aloud, and then stopped himself. He was about to break the rule. The rule was that he couldn't think about things that would happen after his dad got back. And since his dad could be back at any moment, Gregor didn't allow himself to think about the future at all. He had this weird feeling that if he imagined actual events, like having his dad back next Christmas or his dad helping to coach the track team, they would never happen. Besides, as happy as some daydream would make him, it only made returning to reality more painful. So, that was the rule. Gregor had to keep his mind in the present and leave the future to itself. He realized that his system wasn't great, but it was the best way he'd figured out to get through a day.

Gregor noticed that Boots had been suspiciously quiet. He looked around and felt alarmed when he couldn't spot her right away. Then he saw a scuffed pink sandal poking out from the last dryer. "Boots! Get out of there!" said Gregor.

You had to watch her around electrical stuff. She loved plugs.

As he hurried across the laundry room, Gregor heard a metallic klunk and then a giggle from Boots. "Great, now she's dismantling the dryer," thought Gregor, picking up speed. As he reached the far wall, a strange scene confronted him.

The metal grate to an old air duct was wide open, secured by two rusty hinges at the top. Boots was squinting into the opening, about two feet by two feet, which led into the wall of the building. From where he stood, Gregor could see nothing but blackness. Then a wisp of . . . what was it?

Steam? Smoke? It didn't really look like either. Some strange vapor drifted out of the hole and curled around Boots. She held out her arms curiously and leaned forward.

"No!" yelled Gregor as he lunged for her, but Boots's tiny frame seemed to be sucked into the air duct. Without thinking, Gregor thrust his head and shoulders into the hole. The metal grate smacked into his back. The next thing he knew, he was falling down, down, down into empty space.

CHAPTER

2

Gregor twisted around in the air, trying to position himself so he wouldn't land on Boots when they hit the basement floor, but no impact came. Then he remembered the laundry room was in the basement. So what exactly had they fallen into?

The wisps of vapor had thickened into a dense mist that generated a pale light. Gregor could see only a few feet in any direction. His fingers clawed desperately through the white stuff, looking for a handhold, but came up empty. He was plummeting downward so fast, his clothes ballooned around him.

"Boots!" he hollered, and the sound bounced eerily back to him. "There must be sides to this thing," he thought. He called again, "Boots!"

A bright giggle came from somewhere below him. "Ge-go go wheee!" said Boots.

"She thinks she's on a big slide or something," thought Gregor. "At least she's not scared." He felt scared enough for the both of them. Whatever strange hole they had slipped into, it must have a bottom. There was only one way that this spinning through space could end.

Time was passing. Gregor couldn't tell exactly how much, but too much to make sense. Surely there was a limit to how deep a hole could be. At some point, you'd have to run into water or rock or the earth's platelets or something.

It was all like this horrible dream he had sometimes. He'd be up high, somewhere he wasn't supposed to be, usually like the roof of his school. As he walked along the edge, the solid matter under his feet would suddenly give way, and down he'd go. Everything would disappear but the sensation of falling, of the ground closing in on him, of terror. Then, just at the moment of impact, he'd jerk awake, soaked in sweat, heart pounding.

"A dream! I fell asleep in the laundry room and this is the same old crazy dream!" thought Gregor. "Of course! What else could it be?"

Calmed by the notion that he was asleep, Gregor began to gauge his fall. He didn't own a wristwatch, but anybody could count seconds.

"One Mississippi . . . two Mississippi . . . three Mississippi . . ." At seventy Mississippi he gave up and began to feel panicky again. Even in a dream you had to land, didn't you?

Just then, Gregor noticed the mist beginning to clear a little. He could make out the smooth, dark sides of a circular wall. He seemed to be falling down a large, dark tube. He felt an updraft rising from below him. The last wisps of vapor blew away, and Gregor lost speed. His clothes gently settled back on his body.

Below him, he heard a small thump and then the patter of Boots's sandals. A few moments later, his own feet made contact with solid ground. He tried to get his bearings, not daring to move. Total darkness surrounded him. As his eyes adjusted, he became aware of a faint shaft of light off to his left.

A happy squeak came from behind it. "Bug! Beeg bug!"

Gregor ran toward the light. It leaked through a narrow crevice between two smooth walls of rock. He barely managed to squeeze himself through the opening. His sneaker caught on something, causing him to lose his balance. He tripped out from between the rock walls and landed on his hands and knees.

When he raised his head, Gregor found himself looking into the face of the largest cockroach he'd ever seen.

Now, his apartment complex had some big bugs. Mrs. Cormaci claimed a water bug the size of her hand had climbed out of her bathtub drain, and nobody doubted her. But the creature in front of Gregor rose at least four feet in the air. Granted, it was sitting up on its back legs, a very unnatural-looking position for a cockroach, but still . . .

"Beeg bug!" cried Boots again, and Gregor managed to close his mouth. He pushed back onto his knees but he still had to tilt his head back to see the roach. It was holding some kind of torch. Boots scampered over to Gregor and tugged on the neck of his shirt. "Beeeeg bug!" she insisted.

"Yes, I see, Boots. Big bug!" said Gregor in a hushed voice, wrapping his arms tightly around her. "Very . . . big . . . bug."

He tried hard to remember what cockroaches ate. Garbage, rotten food . . . people? He didn't think they ate people. Not the little ones, anyway. Maybe they wanted to eat people but they kept getting stepped on first. At any rate, this wasn't a good time to find out.

Trying to appear casual, Gregor slowly edged his way back toward the crack in the rocks. "Okay, Mr. Roach, so we'll just be going, sorry we bugged you — I mean, bothered you, I mean —"

"Smells what so good, smells what?" a voice hissed, and it took Gregor a full minute to realize it had come from the cockroach. He was too stunned to make any sense of the strange words.

"Uh . . . excuse me?" he managed.

"Smells what so good, smells what?" the voice hissed again, but the tone wasn't threatening. Just curious, and maybe a little excited. "Be small human, be?"

"All right, okay, I'm talking to a giant cockroach," thought Gregor. "Be cool, be nice, answer the bug. He wants to know 'Smells what so good, smells what?' So, tell him." Gregor forced himself to take a deep sniff and then regretted it. Only one thing smelled like that.

"I poop!" said Boots, as if on cue. "I poop, Ge-go!"

"My sister needs a clean diaper," said Gregor, somehow feeling embarrassed.

The roach, if he could read it right, acted impressed.

"Ahhh. Closer come can we, closer come?" said the roach, delicately sweeping the space in front of it with a leg.

"We?" said Gregor. Then he saw the other forms rising out of the dark around them. The smooth black bumps he had taken for rocks were actually the backs of another dozen or so enormous cockroaches. They clustered around Boots eagerly, waving their antennas in the air and shuddering in delight.

Boots, who loved any kind of compliment, instinctively knew she was being admired. She stretched out her chubby arms to the giant insects. "I poop," she said graciously, and they gave an appreciative hiss.

"Be she princess, Overlander, be she? Be she queen, be she?" asked the leader, dipping its head in slavish devotion.

"Boots? A queen?" asked Gregor. Suddenly he had to laugh.

The sound seemed to rattle the roaches, and they withdrew stiffly. "Laugh why, Overlander, laugh why?" one hissed, and Gregor realized he had offended them.

"Because, we're, like, poor and she's kind of a mess and . . . are you calling me Overlander?" he wound up lamely.

"Be you not Overlander human, be you? No Underlander you," said the torchbearing roach peering closely at him. "You look much like but smell not like."

Something seemed to dawn on the leader. "Rat bad." It turned to its comrades. "Leave we Overlanders here, leave we?" The roaches drew closely together in consultation and all began to talk at once.

15

Gregor caught snippets of their conversation, but nothing that made sense. They were so immersed in their debate that he thought about trying to escape again. He looked at his surroundings. In the dim torchlight, they appeared to be in a long, flat tunnel. "We need to go back up," thought Gregor. "Not sideways." He could never scale the walls of the hole they'd fallen down with Boots in his arms.

The roaches came to a decision. "You come, Overlanders. Take to humans," said the leader.

"Humans?" said Gregor, feeling relieved. "There are other humans down here?"

"Ride you, ride you? Run you, run you?" asked the roach, and Gregor understood it was offering him a lift. It didn't look sturdy enough to carry him, but he knew some insects, like ants, could carry many times their weight. He had a sickening image of trying to sit on the roach and crushing it.

"I think I'll walk — I mean, run," said Gregor.

"Ride the princess, ride she?" said the roach hopefully, waving its antennas ingratiatingly and flattening itself on its stomach before Boots. Gregor would have said no, but the toddler climbed right up on the roach's back. He should have known. She loved to sit on the giant metal turtles at the Central Park Zoo.

"Okay, but she has to hold my hand," said Gregor, and Boots obediently latched on to his finger.

The roach took off immediately, and Gregor found himself jogging to keep up with it. He knew roaches could move fast; he'd watched his mother swat enough of them.

Apparently these giant roaches had maintained their speed with their size. Fortunately the floor of the tunnel was even, and Gregor had only finished up track a few weeks ago. He adjusted his pace to match the roaches and soon found a comfortable rhythm.

The tunnel began to twist and turn. The roaches veered into side passages and even doubled back to choose a new route sometimes. In minutes, Gregor was hopelessly lost, and the mental picture of their path that he'd been making in his head resembled one of Boots's squiggly drawings. He gave up trying to remember directions and concentrated on keeping up with the insects. "Man," he thought, "these bugs can really move!"

Gregor began to pant, but the roaches didn't show any visible signs of exertion. He had no idea how far they were going. Their destination could be a hundred miles away. Who knew how far these things could run?

Just when he was about to tell them he needed to rest, Gregor heard a familiar roar. At first he thought he was mistaken, but as they drew closer he felt sure. It was a crowd and, judging by the sound of it, a big one. But where could you fit a crowd in these tunnels?

The floor began to slope sharply, and Gregor found himself backpedaling to avoid stepping on the roach leader. Something soft and feathery brushed against his face and arms. Fabric? Wings? He passed through the stuff, and the unexpected light nearly blinded him. His hand instinctively covered his eyes as they tried to adjust.

A gasp went up from a crowd. He'd been right about that

part. Then it got unnaturally quiet, and he had the sense that a great number of people were looking at him.

Gregor began to make out his surroundings. It wasn't really that bright — in fact, it seemed like evening — but he'd been in darkness so long, he couldn't tell. The first thing he made out was the ground, which appeared to be covered with a dusky green moss. Except it wasn't uneven, but smooth as pavement. He could feel its springiness under his feet. "It's a field," he thought. "For some kind of game. That's why there's a crowd. I'm in a stadium."

Slowly it came into focus. A polished wall enclosed a large oval cavern about fifty feet high. The top of the oval was ringed with bleachers. Gregor's eyes traveled up the distant rows of people as he tried to find the ceiling. Instead, he found the athletes.

A dozen bats were slowly spiraling around the top of the arena. They ranged in color from light yellow to black. Gregor guessed the smallest one had a wingspan of about fifteen feet. The crowd must have been watching them when he stumbled in, because the rest of the field area was empty. "Maybe it's like Rome, and they feed people to the bats. Maybe that's why the roaches brought us here," he thought.

Something fell from one of the bats. It hit the ground in the middle of the stadium and bounced fifty feet into the air. He thought, "Oh, it's just a —"

"Ball!" cried Boots, and before he could stop her she had slid off the roach, wiggled through the other bugs, and started to run across the mossy ground with her little flat-footed stride.

"Most graceful, the princess," hissed a roach dreamily as Gregor headed after her. The insects had shifted easily to let Boots by, but they were an obstacle course for him. Either they were intentionally trying to slow him down, or they were so taken with Boots's beauty that they had forgotten about him entirely.

The ball hit the ground a second time and bounced back in the air. Boots ran after it, reaching her arms high above her head to follow its path.

As Gregor broke free of the roaches and ran for his sister, a shadow passed over him. He looked up and to his horror saw a golden bat diving straight down at Boots. He'd never reach her in time. "Boots!" he screamed, feeling his stomach contract.

She turned around to him and saw the bat for the first time. Her face lit up like a Christmas tree. "Bat!" she shouted, pointing at the monstrous animal above her.

"Geez!" thought Gregor. "Doesn't anything scare her?"

The bat swooped over Boots, lightly brushing her finger with its belly fur, and then soared back into the air in a loop. At the top of the arc, while the bat was flat on its back, Gregor noticed for the first time that someone was sitting on it. The rider had its legs wrapped around the bat's neck. He realized it was a girl.

The upside-down girl released her legs and dropped off the bat's back. She executed a perfect double back-flip, twisting around at the last moment to face Gregor's direction, and landed on the ground as lightly as a cat in front of Boots. One hand went out, and the ball fell into it in what was either a feat of remarkable timing or incredible luck.

Gregor looked at the girl's face and could tell by her arrogant expression that there had been no luck involved at all.

CHAPTER

3

Hands down, she was the strangest-looking person Gregor had ever seen. Her skin was so pale, he could see every vein in her body. He thought of the section on the human anatomy in his science book. Flip one page, see the bones. Next, the digestive system. This girl was a walking circulatory system.

At first he thought her hair was gray like his grandma's, but that wasn't right. It was really more of a silver color, like blond hair with a metallic tint. The hair was woven in an intricate braid down her back and was tucked into a belt at her waist. A thin band of gold encircled the girl's head. It could have been some kind of hair band, but Gregor had a bad feeling it was a crown.

He didn't want this girl to be in charge. He could tell by the upright way she held herself, by the slight smile at the left corner of her mouth, by the way she managed to be looking down at him even though he was a good six inches taller than she was, that she had real attitude. That's what his mom would say about certain girls he knew. "She's got real attitude." She would shake her head, but Gregor could tell she approved of these girls.

Well, there was having attitude and then there was just being a total show-off.

Gregor felt sure she'd done that fancy trick off the bat completely for his benefit. One flip would have been plenty. It was her way to intimidate him, but he wouldn't be intimidated. Gregor looked straight into the girl's eyes and saw that her irises were a dazzling shade of light purple. He held his ground.

Gregor didn't know how long they might have stood there sizing each other up if Boots hadn't intervened. She plowed into the girl, knocking her off balance. The girl staggered back a step and looked at Boots in disbelief.

Boots grinned winningly and held up a pudgy hand. "Ball?" she said hopefully.

The girl knelt on one knee and held out the ball to Boots, but she kept her fingers wrapped tightly around it. "It is yours if you can take it," she said in a voice like her eyes: cold, and clear, and foreign.

Boots tried to take the ball, but the girl didn't release it. Confused, she pulled on the girl's fingers. "Ball?"

The girl shook her head. "You will have to be stronger or smarter than I am."

Boots looked up at the girl, registered something, and poked her right in the eye. "Pu-ple!" she said. The girl jerked back, dropping the ball. Boots scrambled after it and scooped it up.

Gregor couldn't resist. "I guess she's smarter," he said. It was a little mean, but he didn't like her messing with Boots that way.

The girl narrowed her eyes. "But not you. Or you would not say such things to a queen."

So, he had been right: She was royalty. Now she'd probably chop off his head or something. Still, he felt it would be bad if he acted scared. Gregor shrugged. "No, if I'd known you were a queen, I'd probably have said something a lot cooler."

"Cool-er?" she said, raising her eyebrows.

"Better," said Gregor, for lack of a cooler word.

The girl decided to take it as an apology. "I will forgive it as you are not knowing. What are you called, Overlander?"

"My name's Gregor. And that's Boots," he said, pointing to his sister. "Well, her name's not really Boots, it's Margaret, but we call her Boots because in the winter she steals everybody's boots and runs around in them and because of this musician my dad likes." That sounded confusing even to Gregor. "What's your name?"

"I am Queen Luxa," said the girl.

"Louk-za?" said Gregor, trying to get the odd inflection right.

"What means this, what the baby says? Pu-ple?" she asked.

"Purple. It's her favorite color. And your eyes, she's never seen purple eyes before," explained Gregor.

Boots heard the word and came over holding up her palms, which were still dyed purple from the marker. "Pu-ple!"

"I have never seen brown before. Not on a human," said Luxa, staring into Boots's eyes. "Or this." She caught Boots's wrist and ran her fingers over the silky, light brown skin. "It must need much light."

Boots giggled. Every inch of her was ticklish. Luxa purposely ran her fingers up under Boots's chin, making her laugh. For a second, Luxa lost her attitude, and Gregor thought she might not be so bad. Then she straightened up and resumed her haughty manner. "So, Gregor the Overlander, you and the baby must bathe."

Gregor knew he was sweaty from running through the tunnels, but that was pretty rude. "Maybe we should just go."

"Go? Go where?" asked Luxa in surprise.

"Home," he said.

"Smelling like you do?" said Luxa. "You will be thrice dead before you reach the Waterway, even if you knew the path to take." She could see he didn't understand. "You smell of the Overland. That is not safe for you here. Or for us."

"Oh," said Gregor, feeling a little foolish. "I guess we should rinse off before we go home, then."

"It is not so simple. But I will let Vikus explain," said Luxa. "You have had rare luck today, being found so quickly."

"How do you know we were found quickly?" asked Gregor.

"Our lookouts noted you shortly after you landed. As you were the crawlers' find, we let them present you," she said.

"I see," said Gregor. Where had the lookouts been? Concealed in the gloom of the tunnels? Hidden somewhere in the mist he'd fallen through? Until the stadium, he hadn't seen anyone but the roaches.

"These were headed here, in any case," she said, gesturing to the roaches. "See, they carry torches. They would not bother if they were not visiting us."

"Why's that?" said Gregor.

"Crawlers do not need light. But they show themselves to us to let us know they come peacefully. Did you not wonder at how easily you arrived here?" she asked. Without waiting for an answer, she turned to the group of cockroaches who had been standing patiently off to the side. "Crawlers, what take you for the Overlanders?"

The head roach scurried forward. "Give you five baskets, give you?" he hissed.

"We will give three grain baskets," said Luxa.

"Rats give many fish," said the roach, cleaning its antennas casually.

"Take them to the rats, then. It will give you no time," said Luxa.

Gregor didn't know exactly what they were talking about, but he had the uneasy sense he was for sale.

The insect considered Luxa's last offer. "Give you four baskets, give you?" it said.

25

"We will give four baskets, and one for thanks," said a voice behind Gregor. He turned and saw a pale, bearded man approaching them on foot. His close-cropped hair really was silver, not just the silvery blond.

Luxa glared at the old man but didn't contradict him.

The cockroach painstakingly added up four and one on its legs. "Give you five baskets, give you?" it asked, as if the whole idea was a new one.

"We will give five baskets," said Luxa less than graciously, giving the roach a terse bow. It bowed back and scampered off with the other bugs out of the stadium.

"And if it is up to Vikus, soon we will have no baskets to give," the girl said pointedly to the bearded man who had turned his focus to Gregor and Boots.

"One more basket will be a small price to pay if he is expected," he answered. His violet eyes stared intently at Gregor. "Tell me, Overlander, are you from . . ." He searched for the words. "New York City?"

CHAPTER

It was as if someone had splashed water in Gregor's face and brought reality rushing back. Ever since he'd fallen through the hole in the wall, things had been happening so fast, it was all he could do to keep up with them. Now, in this momentary calm, the words "New York City" came as a shock.

Yes! He was a kid who lived in New York City and had to do the laundry and get back upstairs with his little sister before his mother — *his mother*!

"I have to get home now!" Gregor blurted out.

His mom worked as a receptionist at a dentist's office. She usually got off right at five and was home by five-thirty. She'd be worried sick if she came in and found that he and Boots had disappeared. Especially after what had happened to his dad. He tried to figure out how much time had passed since he was in the laundry room. "We probably fell for, let's say, five minutes and then we must have run for about twenty with the roaches and we've been here maybe ten," he thought. Thirty-five minutes.

"Okay, so the clothes should be about dry!" he said aloud. "If we get back up there in the next twenty minutes it should be okay." No one would think to look for them before that, and he could just take the laundry up and fold it in the apartment.

"Really, I need to go back up right now," he said to Vikus.

The old man was still examining him closely. "It is simple to fall down, but the going up requires much giving."

"What do you mean?" asked Gregor, his throat tightening.

"He means you cannot go home," said Luxa flatly. "You must stay with us in the Underland."

"Uh, no! No, thank you!" said Gregor. "I mean, you're all great, but I've got stuff to do . . . upstairs!" he said. "Thanks again! Nice meeting you! Come on, Boots!"

Gregor scooped up his sister and headed for the arched opening the roaches had left by. Out of the corner of his eye he saw Luxa raise her hand. For a moment he thought she was waving good-bye, but that couldn't be right. Luxa wasn't friendly enough to wave. "If it's not a wave, then it's a signal!" he muttered to Boots. Then he bolted for the doorway.

He might have made it if he hadn't been hauling Boots, but he couldn't really run with her in his arms. Ten yards from the exit the first bat swept in front of him, knocking him flat on his back on the ground. His body cushioned

Boots's fall, and she immediately sat up on his stomach to enjoy the show.

Every bat in the arena had dived for them. They flew in a tight circle around Gregor and Boots, locking them in a prison of wings and fur. Each one had a rider as pale and silver-haired as Luxa. Despite the close proximity and speed of the bats, none of the people had any trouble staying mounted. In fact, only a few bothered to hold on at all. One cocky-looking guy on a glossy black bat actually lay in a reclining position, propping up his head with one hand.

The riders couldn't take their eyes off the captives. As they flashed by, Gregor could see their expressions ranged from amusement to outright hostility.

Boots bounced on his stomach and clapped her tiny hands. "Bats! Bats! Bats! Bats!"

"Well, at least one of us is enjoying this," thought Gregor.

Boots loved bats. At the zoo, she'd stand in front of the large plate-glass window of the bat habitat forever if you let her. In the small, dark display, hundreds of bats managed to flit around continuously without knocking into one another. They could do that because of something called echolocation. The bats would emit a sound that would echo off something solid and they'd be able to tell where it was located. Gregor had read the card on echolocation about a billion times waiting for Boots to get tired of the bats. He felt like something of an expert on the subject.

"Bats! Bats! Bats!" chanted Boots, using his stomach for a trampoline. Feeling queasy, Gregor pushed himself up on his elbows and scooted her onto the ground. The last thing he needed was to throw up in front of these people.

He got to his feet. Boots tucked her arm around his knee and leaned against him. The circle of bats shrunk in even closer. "What? Like I'm going somewhere?" said Gregor with aggravation. He heard a couple of the riders laugh.

Luxa must have given another signal, because the bats peeled off one at a time and began wheeling around the arena in complicated patterns. Gregor saw that neither she nor Vikus had bothered to move from where he had left them. He looked at the doorway and he knew it was pointless. Still . . . these people were a little too smug for their own good.

Gregor sprinted three steps for the exit before he whipped around and headed back to Luxa, catching his sister's hand on the way. Taken by surprise, the bats broke out of their formation and zoomed down, only to find themselves with no one to capture. They pulled up in an awkward clump, and while they didn't actually collide, Gregor felt gratified to see several riders struggling to stay on their bats.

The crowd, which had been amazingly quiet since their appearance, broke out in appreciative laughter. Gregor felt a little more confident. At least he wasn't the only one who'd looked like an idiot. "Faked them out," he said to Boots.

Luxa's gaze was icy, but Gregor saw Vikus trying to suppress a smile as he walked up. "So, you said something about a bath?" he said to Luxa.

"You will follow to the palace *now*," said Luxa crossly. She flicked her hand, and her golden bat swept down behind her. Just as it was about to crash into her, Luxa leaped in the air. She lifted her legs straight out to the sides and touched her toes in a move Gregor thought he'd maybe seen cheerleaders do. The bat ducked under her, and she landed on its back easily. It arched up, missing Gregor by inches. Then it righted itself in the air and sped out of the stadium.

"You're wasting your time with that stuff!" called Gregor, although Luxa was out of earshot. He felt angry with himself because, in fact, he had to admit this girl had some moves.

Vikus had heard him, though. His smile broadened. Gregor scowled at the old man. "What?"

"Will you follow to the palace, Overlander?" asked Vikus politely.

"As what, your prisoner?" said Gregor bluntly.

"As our guest, I hope," replied Vikus. "Although Queen Luxa has no doubt ordered the dungeon readied for you." His violet eyes literally twinkled, and Gregor found himself liking the man in spite of himself. Maybe because he was pretty sure Vikus liked him. He resisted the temptation to smile.

"Lead the way," said Gregor indifferently.

Vikus nodded and waved him toward the far side of the arena. Gregor followed a few steps behind him, towing Boots.

The stands were beginning to empty. High in the air, the people filed out through exits between their bleachers. Several bats still wove around the stadium doing aerodynamic maneuvers. Whatever game had been in progress had ended when Gregor arrived. The remaining bats and riders were hanging around to keep an eye on him.

As they neared the main entrance of the stadium, Vikus dropped back and fell in step with Gregor. "You must feel as if you are trapped in a dream, Overlander."

"I was thinking nightmare," said Gregor evenly.

Vikus chuckled. "Our bats and crawlers — no, what is it you call them? Cockhorses?"

"Cockroaches," corrected Gregor.

"Ah, yes, cockroaches," agreed Vikus. "In the Overland, they are but handfuls while here they grow largely."

"How do you know that? Have you been to the Overland?" said Gregor. If Vikus could get there, then so could he and Boots.

"Oh, no, such visits are as rare as trees. It is the Overlanders who come at times to us. I have met six or seven. One called Fred Clark, another called Mickey, and most recently a woman known as Coco. What are you called, Overlander?" asked Vikus.

"Gregor. Are they still here? Are the other Overlanders still here?" asked Gregor, brightening at the thought.

"Sadly, no. This is not a gentle place for Overlanders," said Vikus, his face darkening.

Gregor stopped, pulling Boots up short. "You mean you killed them?"

Now he'd insulted the guy.

"We? We humans kill the Overlanders? I know of your

world, of the evils that transpire there. But we do not kill for sport!" said Vikus severely. "Today we have taken you in among us. Had we denied you, count on it, you would not be breathing now!"

"I didn't mean you . . . I mean, I didn't know how it worked here," stammered Gregor. Although he should have guessed that it wasn't very diplomatic to suggest Vikus was a murderer. "So, the roaches would have killed us?"

"The crawlers kill you?" said Vikus. "No, it would give them no time."

There was that expression again. What did it mean to give the roaches time?

"But no one else even knows we're here," said Gregor.

Vikus looked at him gravely. Concern had replaced his anger. "Believe me, boy, by this time, every creature in the Underland knows you are here."

Gregor resisted an impulse to look over his shoulder. "And that's not a good thing, is it?"

Vikus shook his head. "No. That is not in any manner a good thing."

The old man turned to the exit of the stadium. Half a dozen pale, violet-eyed guards flanked two gigantic stone doors. It took their combined efforts to push the doors open a few feet and to allow Vikus to pass.

Gregor led Boots through the doors, and they closed immediately behind him. He followed Vikus down a tunnel lined with stone torches to a small arch filled with something dark and fluttery. Gregor thought it might be more bats, but on closer inspection he saw it was a cloud of tiny black moths. Was this what he had passed through when he stumbled into the stadium?

Vikus gently slid his hand into the insects. "These moths are a warning system peculiar to the Underland, I believe. The moment their pattern of flight is disturbed by an intruder, every bat in the area discerns it. I find it so perfect in its simplicity," he said. Then he vanished into the moths.

Behind the curtain of wings, Gregor could hear his voice beckoning. "Gregor the Overlander, welcome to the city of Regalia!"

Gregor glanced down at Boots, who had a puzzled look on her face. "Go home, Ge-go?" she asked.

He picked her up and gave her what he hoped was a reassuring hug. "Not now, baby. We have to do some things first. Then we'll go home."

Gregor took a deep breath and stepped into the moths.

CHAPTER

5

The velvety wings brushed past his cheek, and he caught his first sight of Regalia. "Wow!" he said, stopping in his tracks.

Gregor didn't know what he'd expected. Maybe stone houses, maybe caves — something primitive. But there was nothing primitive about the magnificent city that spread before him.

They stood on the edge of a valley filled with the most beautiful buildings he'd ever seen. New York was known for its architecture, the elegant brownstones, the towering skyscrapers, the grand museums. But compared with Regalia, it looked unplanned, like a place where someone had lined up a bunch of oddly shaped boxes in rows.

The buildings here were all a lovely misty gray, which

gave them a dreamlike quality. They seemed to rise directly out of the rock as if they had been grown, not made by human hands. Maybe they weren't as tall as the skyscrapers Gregor knew by name, but they towered high above his head, some at least thirty stories and finished in artful peaks and turrets. Thousands of torches were placed strategically so that a soft, dusky light illuminated the entire city.

And the carvings . . . Gregor had seen cherubs and gargoyles on buildings before, but the walls of Regalia crawled with life. People and cockroaches and fish and creatures Gregor had no name for fought and feasted and danced on every conceivable inch of space.

"Do just people live here, or roaches and bats, too?" asked Gregor.

"This is a city of humans. The others have their own cities, or perhaps 'lands' might be a more accurate word," said Vikus. "The majority of our people live here, although some dwell in the suburbs, if their work so dictates. There stands our palace," said Vikus, directing Gregor's eye to a huge, circular fortress at the far edge of the valley. "There we are headed."

The lights shining from the city's many windows gave it a festive look, and Gregor felt his heart lightening a little. New York City glittered all night long, too. Maybe this place wasn't so foreign after all.

"It's really great," he said. He would have loved to explore it, if he didn't need to get home so badly.

"Yes," said Vikus, as his eyes took in the city fondly. "My

people have much love of stone. Had we time, I think we might create a land of rare beauty."

"I think maybe you already have," said Gregor. "I mean, it's way more beautiful than anything in the Overland."

Vikus seemed pleased. "Come, the palace has the fairest view of the city. You will have time to admire before we dine."

As Gregor followed him down the road, Boots tilted back her head, turning it from side to side. "What'd you lose, Boots?"

"Moon?" said Boots. Usually you couldn't see the stars from where they lived, but the moon was visible on clear nights. "Moon?"

Gregor looked up into the inky black sky and then realized that, of course, there was no sky. They were in some kind of gigantic underground cavern. "No moon, little girl. No moon tonight," he said.

"Cow jump moon," she said matter-of-factly.

"Mm-hm," agreed Gregor. If roaches talked, and bats played ball games, then probably there was a cow jumping a moon somewhere, too. He sighed as he pictured the tattered nursery rhyme book in the box by Boots's crib at home.

People stared openly at them from the windows as they passed. Vikus acknowledged a few, nodding or calling out a name, and they'd raise their hands in greeting back.

Boots noticed and began to wave. "Hi!" she called. "Hi!" and while none of the adults answered her, Gregor saw a few little kids wave back.

"You hold great fascination for them," said Vikus, indicating the people in the windows. "We do not get many visits from the Overland."

"How did you know I was from New York?" asked Gregor.

"There are but five known gateways to the Underland," said Vikus. "Two lead to the Dead Land, but you would never have survived those. Two gateways open into the Waterway, but your clothing is quite dry. You are alive, you are dry, from this I surmise you have fallen through the fifth gateway, the mouth of which I know to be in New York City."

"It's in my laundry room!" Gregor blurted out. "Right in our apartment building!" Somehow the fact that his laundry room connected to this strange place made him feel invaded.

"Your laundry room, yes," said Vikus thoughtfully. "Well, your fall coincided most favorably with the currents."

"The currents? You mean that misty stuff?" asked Gregor.

"Yes, they allowed you to arrive here in one piece. Timing is all," said Vikus.

"What happens if the timing is off?" asked Gregor, but he already knew the answer.

"Then we have a body to bury instead of a guest," said Vikus quietly. "That, in truth, is the most common outcome. A living Overlander like yourself, plus your sister, well, this is most singular."

It took a good twenty minutes to reach the palace, and Gregor's arms began to tremble from carrying Boots.

Somehow he didn't want to put her down. It didn't seem safe with all the torches around.

As they approached the magnificent structure, Gregor noticed there was nothing carved on it. The sides were as smooth as glass, and the lowest window opened two hundred feet above the ground. Something was off, but he couldn't quite place it. Something was missing. "There's no door," he said aloud.

"No," said Vikus. "Doors are for those who lack enemies. Even the most accomplished climber cannot find a foothold here."

Gregor ran his hand along the polished stone wall. There wasn't a crack, not even the tiniest nick in the surface. "So, how do you get inside?"

"We usually fly, but if one's bat cannot accommodate . . ." Vikus gestured above his head. Gregor craned his neck back and saw that a platform was being rapidly lowered from a large, rectangular window. It caught on the ropes that supported it about a foot from the ground, and Vikus stepped aboard.

Gregor climbed on with Boots. His recent fall to the Underland had only reinforced how much he disliked heights. The platform immediately rose, and he grabbed hold of the side rope to steady himself. Vikus stood calmly with his hands folded before him, but then Vikus wasn't holding a wiggly two-year-old, and he'd probably ridden this thing a million times.

The ascent was rapid and even. The platform leveled off at the window before a small, stone staircase. Gregor carried

Boots inside a large room with vaulted ceilings. A group of three Underlanders, all with the same translucent skin and violet eyes, waited to greet them.

"Good late day," said Vikus, nodding to the Underlanders. "Meet you Gregor and Boots the Overlanders, brother and sister, who have most recently fallen among us. Please bathe them and then proceed to the High Hall." Without a backward glance, Vikus strode out of the room.

Gregor and the Underlanders stared awkwardly at one another. None of them had Luxa's arrogance or Vikus's easy commanding presence. "They're just regular people," he thought. "I bet they feel as weird as I do."

"Nice to meet you," he said, shifting Boots over to his other hip. "Say hi, Boots."

"Hi!" said Boots, waving at the Underlanders and looking completely delighted. "Hi! Hi, you!"

The Underlanders' reserve melted like butter in a skillet. They all laughed, and the stiffness went out of their bodies. Gregor found himself laughing, too. His mom said Boots never knew a stranger, which meant she thought everybody in the world was her friend.

Gregor sometimes wished he could be more like that. He had a couple of good friends, but he avoided becoming part of any one clique at school. It all came down to who you ate lunch with. He could've sat with the guys he ran track with. Or the band kids. But instead he liked being with Angelina, who was always in some school play, and Larry, who just . . . well, mostly he just drew stuff. Some people who didn't really know him thought Gregor was stuck-up, but he was mostly just private. He had more trouble opening up to people after his dad left. But even before that, he'd never been as friendly as Boots.

A young woman who looked about fifteen stepped forward and held out her arms. "I am called Dulcet. May I take you, Boots? You would care for a bath?" Boots looked at Gregor for confirmation.

"It's okay. Bath-time. You want a bath, Boots?" he asked.

"Ye-es!" cried Boots happily. "Bath!" She reached out for Dulcet, who took her from Gregor's arms.

"Meet you Mareth and Perdita," said Dulcet, indicating the man and woman next to her. They were both tall and muscular and, although they didn't carry weapons, Gregor had a feeling they were guards.

"Hey," he said.

Mareth and Perdita both gave him formal, but friendly, nods.

Dulcet wrinkled her nose and poked Boots gently in the tummy. "You have need of a clean catch cloth," she said.

Gregor could guess what a catch cloth was. "Oh, yeah, her diaper needs to be changed." It had been a while. "She's going to get a rash."

"I poop!" said Boots without apology, and tugged on her diaper.

"I will attend to it," said Dulcet with an amused smile, and Gregor couldn't help thinking how much nicer she was than Luxa. "You will follow to the waters, Gregor the Overlander?"

"Yes, thank you, I will follow to the waters," said Gregor.

He was struck by how formal he sounded and he didn't want the Underlanders to think he was making fun of them. The roaches had been so easy to insult. "I mean, yeah, thanks."

Dulcet nodded and waited for him to fall in step beside her. Mareth and Perdita followed a few steps behind. "They're guards, all right," thought Gregor.

The group left the entrance room and walked down a spacious hallway. They passed dozens of arched doorways that opened into large chambers, staircases, and halls. Gregor quickly realized he'd need a map to navigate the place. He could ask directions, but that wouldn't be too smart if he was trying to escape. They could call him their guest, but it didn't change the fact that he and Boots were prisoners. Guests could leave if they wanted to. Prisoners had to escape. And that was exactly what he intended to do.

But how? Even if he could find his way back to the platform, no one would let him down, and he couldn't jump two hundred feet to the ground. "But there must be other ways to enter the palace," he thought. "There must be —"

"I have never met an Overlander before," said Dulcet, interrupting his train of thought. "It is only because of the baby I meet you now."

"Because of Boots?" said Gregor.

"I take care of the young ones for many," said Dulcet. "I would not usually meet so important a person as an Overlander," she said shyly.

"Well, that's too bad, Dulcet," said Gregor, "because you're the nicest person I've met here yet."

Dulcet blushed, and boy, when these people blushed, they really blushed! Her skin turned pink as ripe watermelon. Not just her face, either; she colored to the tips of her fingers.

"Oh," she stammered, very embarrassed. "Oh, that is too kind for me to accept." Behind him, the two guards murmured something to each other.

Gregor guessed he had said something way out of line, but he didn't know what. Maybe you weren't supposed to imply a nanny was nicer than the queen. Even if it was true. He was going to have to be more careful about what he said.

Fortunately, just then they stopped at a doorway. He could hear water running, and steam wafted out into the hall.

"Must be the bathroom," he thought. He looked inside and saw that a wall divided the room into two sections.

"I will take Boots, and you go in here," said Dulcet, indicating one side.

Gregor guessed it must be girls on one side, boys on the other, like locker rooms. He thought maybe he should stay with Boots, but he felt as if he could trust Dulcet, and he didn't want to upset her again. "Okay, Boots? See you soon?"

"Bye-bye!" waved Boots over Dulcet's shoulder. Clearly she wasn't having any separation anxiety.

Gregor veered off to the right. The place did kind of resemble a locker room if locker rooms were gorgeous and smelled good. Exotic sea creatures were carved into the walls, and oil lamps cast a golden glow. "Okay, but it's got benches and lockers, sort of," he thought, taking in the rows of stone benches and the open cubicles that lined one side of the room.

Mareth had followed him in. He addressed Gregor nervously. "This place is the changing room. Here are the rooms for relief and cleansing. Can I get you anything, Gregor the Overlander?"

"No, thanks, I think I can figure it out," said Gregor.

"We shall be in the hall if you have need," said Mareth.

"Okay, thanks a lot," said Gregor. When the Underlander ducked out the door he felt the muscles in his face release. It was good to be alone.

He made a quick inspection of the place. The relief room held only a solid stone chair with an opening cut in the middle. Looking inside, Gregor saw water ran continuously in a stream underneath it. "Oh, it must be the toilet," he thought.

The cleansing room had a small, steaming pool with steps that led down into the water. A fragrant smell filled the air. His whole body ached to get into the water.

Gregor quickly returned to the changing room and stripped off his sweaty clothes. Feeling self-conscious, he peed in the toilet. Then he hurried to the pool. He tested the temperature with his toe and slowly walked down into the steamy water. It reached his waist, but he discovered the pool had a bench around it. When he sat down, the water licked his ears.

A current washed over him, releasing the knots in his shoulders and back. Gregor cut the surface of the pool with his hand, and the water ran through his fingers. Like the water in the toilet, it flowed in one end of the bath and out the other.

"It must be some kind of underground stream," he thought.

He sat straight up as the idea hit him. The water came from somewhere! It went somewhere!

If water could get in and out of the palace . . . maybe he could, too.

CHAPTER

6

Gregor scrubbed himself down using a sponge and some gloopy stuff he found in a bowl by the pool. He lathered his hair and even cleaned inside his ears wanting to get every bit of Overlander smell off him. If he was going to try to escape, he needed to be as indistinguishable from his hosts as possible.

On hooks by the pool hung a row of white towels. Gregor couldn't identify the thick woven fabric. "Sure not cotton," he muttered, but the towel was soft and absorbed water much better than the thin, worn ones they used at home.

He walked back into the changing room drying his hair and found his clothes had disappeared. In their place was a neat pile of smoky blue garments. A shirt, pants, and what seemed to be underwear. They were much finer than the towels — the cloth ran silkily through his fingers. "What is this stuff?" he wondered, slipping into the shirt.

He slid his feet into a pair of braided straw sandals and padded out of the changing room. Mareth and Perdita were waiting.

"So, what happened to my clothes?" asked Gregor.

"They have been burned," said Mareth apprehensively. Gregor sensed Mareth was afraid he'd be mad.

"It is most dangerous to keep them," said Perdita, by way of explanation. "The ash carries no scent."

Gregor shrugged to show he didn't care. "That's cool," he said. "These fit me fine."

Mareth and Perdita looked grateful. "After a few days of our food, you will be without much odor, too," said Perdita encouragingly.

"That'll be nice," said Gregor dryly. These Underlanders were sure obsessed with his smell.

Dulcet emerged from the left side of the bathroom carrying a squeaky clean Boots. She had on a soft, rose-colored shirt, and a clean diaper made from the same material as Gregor's bath towel. She extended her leg and pointed proudly to the new sandal on her foot. "San-da," she said to Gregor.

He stuck out his foot to show her his shoes. "Me, too," he said. He assumed they'd burned Boots's clothes, as well. He tried to remember what she'd been wearing in case he had to explain the missing stuff to his mom. One dirty diaper, no loss. One pair of scuffed pink sandals her feet were growing out of, anyway. One stained T-shirt. It would probably be okay.

Gregor didn't know exactly what he would tell his mom about the Underland. The truth would scare her to death. He'd work out something when they got back to the laundry room, but the sooner that happened, the simpler the story could be.

Boots reached out her arms and Gregor took her, pressing his nose into her damp curls. She smelled fresh and a bit like the ocean.

"She is well grown," said Dulcet. "Your arms must be tired." She went back into the changing room and came out with some kind of pack. It fitted on his back with straps, and Boots could ride in it looking over his shoulder. He had seen people carrying kids in specially designed backpacks, but his family didn't have money for that sort of stuff.

"Thanks," he said casually, but he was secretly elated. It would be a lot easier to escape with Boots in a backpack than in his arms.

Dulcet led them up several staircases and through a maze of halls. They eventually wound up in a long room that opened out on to a balcony.

"We call this the High Hall," said Dulcet.

"I think you guys forgot the roof," said Gregor. While the walls were decorated with the greatest care, there was nothing but the black cavern above their heads.

Dulcet laughed. "Oh, no, it is meant to be so. We entertain here often, and many bats can arrive at once." Gregor imagined the bottleneck a hundred bats would cause trying to get in the door downstairs. He could see the advantage of a bigger landing strip.

Vikus was waiting for them by the balcony with an older woman. Gregor guessed she might be around his grandma's age, but his grandma was stooped and moved painfully from arthritis. This woman stood very straight and looked strong.

"Gregor and Boots the Overlanders, my wife, Solovet," said Vikus.

"Hey," said Gregor, "nice to meet you."

But the woman stepped forward and offered both her hands to him. The gesture surprised him. No one else had made any effort to touch him since he'd landed.

"Welcome, Gregor. Welcome, Boots," she said in a low, warm voice. "It is an honor to have you among us."

"Thanks," Gregor mumbled, confused because she was throwing his prisoner status off balance. She really made him feel like someone special.

"Hi, you!" said Boots, and Solovet reached up to pat her cheek.

"Vikus tells me you are very anxious to return home. It pains me that we cannot aid you immediately, but to seek the surface tonight would be impossible," she said. "The Underland buzzes with news of your arrival."

"I guess everyone wants to look at us, like we're freaks or something. Well, they'd better look fast," thought Gregor. But he said, "Then I'll get to see some stuff down here."

Vikus waved him over to the low wall that ringed the balcony. "Come, come, there is much to view," he said.

Gregor joined Vikus at the wall and felt his stomach lurch. He involuntarily took a few steps backward. The balcony, it seemed, hung out over the side of the palace. Only the floor separated him from the dizzying drop.

"Do not fear, it is well built," said Vikus.

Gregor nodded but didn't move forward again. If the thing started collapsing he wanted to be able to make it back to the High Hall. "I can see fine from here," he said. And he could.

Regalia was even more impressive from above. On the ground, he couldn't see that the streets, which were paved in various shades of stone, were laid out in a complex geometric pattern so that the city looked like a giant mosaic. He also hadn't realized how big the place was. It extended out several miles each direction. "How many people live down here?" asked Gregor.

"We number three thousand or so," said Vikus. "More, if the harvest reaps well."

Three thousand. Gregor tried to get a mental picture of how many people that would be. His school had about six hundred kids in it, so five times that.

"So, what are you guys doing down here, anyway?" asked Gregor.

Vikus laughed. "We are amazed it has taken you so long to ask. Well, it is a marvelous tale," said Vikus, taking a deep breath to begin it. "Once many years ago there lived —"

"Vikus," interrupted Solovet. "Perhaps the tale would go well with supper."

Gregor silently thanked her. He was starving, and he had a feeling Vikus wasn't the kind of guy to leave out any details.

The dining room was off the High Hall. A table had been set for eight. Gregor hoped Dulcet would be joining them, but after tucking Boots in a sort of high chair, she backed up several feet from the table and stood. Gregor didn't feel comfortable eating with her standing there, but he thought he might get her in trouble if he said something.

Neither Vikus nor Solovet took a chair, so Gregor decided to wait, too. Soon Luxa swept into the room in a dress that was a lot fancier than the clothes she'd worn in the stadium. Her hair was loose and fell like a shiny silver sheet to her waist. She was with a guy who Gregor guessed was about sixteen. He was laughing at something she'd just said. Gregor recognized him from the stadium. It was the rider who'd felt cocky enough to lie down on his bat as they'd swirled around his head.

"Another show-off," thought Gregor. But the guy gave him such a friendly look that Gregor decided not to jump to conclusions. Luxa was annoying, but most of the other Underlanders were okay.

"My cousin, Henry," said Luxa shortly, and Gregor wanted to laugh. Here among all these strange names was a Henry.

Henry gave Gregor a low bow and came up grinning. "Welcome, Overlander," he said. Then he grabbed Gregor's arm and spoke in his ear in a dramatically hushed voice. "Beware the fish, for Luxa plans to poison you directly!"

Vikus and Solovet laughed, and even Dulcet smiled. It was a joke. These people actually had a sense of humor.

"Beware *your* fish, Henry," returned Luxa. "I gave orders to poison scoundrels, forgetting you would be dining as well."

Henry winked at Gregor. "Switch plates with the bats," he whispered, and at that moment two bats swooped into the room from the High Hall. "Ah, the bats!"

Gregor recognized the golden bat Luxa had been riding earlier. A large gray bat fluttered into a chair near Vikus, and everyone else took a seat.

"Gregor the Overlander, meet you Aurora and Euripedes. They are bonded to Luxa and myself," said Vikus, extending a flexed hand to the gray bat on his right. Euripedes brushed the hand with his wing. Luxa and her golden bat Aurora performed the same exchange.

Gregor had thought the bats were like horses, but now he could see they were equals. Did they talk?

"Greetings, Overlander," said Euripedes in a soft purring voice.

Yeah, they talked. Gregor began to wonder if his fish dinner would want to chat as he sliced into it.

"Nice to meet you," said Gregor politely. "What does that mean, that you're bonded to each other?"

"Soon after we arrived in the Underland we humans formed a special alliance with the bats," said Solovet. "Both sides saw the obvious advantages to joining together. But beyond our alliance, individual bats and humans may form their own union. That is called bonding."

"And what do you do if you're bonded to a bat?" asked Gregor. "I mean, besides play ball games together."

There was a pause in which glances were exchanged around the table. He'd said something wrong again.

"You keep each other alive," said Luxa coldly.

It had seemed like he was making fun of something serious. "Oh, I didn't know," said Gregor.

"Of course, you did not," said Solovet, shooting a look at Luxa. "You have no parallel in your own land."

"And do you bond with the crawlers, too?" Gregor asked.

Henry snorted with laughter. "I would as soon bond with a stone. At least it could be counted on not to run away in battle."

Luxa broke into a grin. "And perhaps you could throw it. I suppose you could throw a crawler. . . ."

"But then I would have to touch it!" said Henry, and the two cracked up.

"The crawlers are not known for their fighting ability," said Vikus, by way of explanation to Gregor. Neither he nor Solovet were laughing. He turned to Luxa and Henry. "Yet they live on. Perhaps when you can comprehend the reason for their longevity you will have more respect for them."

Henry and Luxa attempted to look serious, although their eyes were still laughing.

"It is of little consequence to the crawlers whether I respect them or not," said Henry lightly.

"Perhaps not, but it is of great consequence whether Luxa does. Or so it will be in some five years when she comes of age to rule," said Vikus. "At that time, foolish jokes at the crawlers' expense may make the difference between our existence and our annihilation. They do not need to be warriors to shift the balance of power in the Underland."

This sobered Luxa up for real, but it killed the conversation. An awkward pause stretched into an embarrassing silence. Gregor thought he understood what Vikus had meant. The crawlers would make better friends than enemies, and humans shouldn't go around insulting them.

To Gregor's relief, the food arrived, and an Underlander servant placed a half circle of small bowls around him. At least three contained what looked like various types of mushrooms. One had a ricelike grain, and the smallest contained a handful of fresh greens. He could tell by the skimpy portion that the leafy stuff was supposed to be a big treat.

A platter with a whole grilled fish was set in front of him. The fish resembled the ones Gregor was used to except it had no eyes. He and his dad had once watched a show on TV about fish that lived way down deep in some cave and didn't have eyes, either. The weird thing was that when the scientists brought some up to study in a lab, the fish had sensed the light and had grown eyes. Not right away, but in a few generations.

His dad had gotten very excited over the show and had taken Gregor to the American Museum of Natural History to look for eyeless fish. They had ended up at the museum a lot, just the two of them. His dad was crazy about science, and it seemed as if he wanted to pour everything in his brain right into Gregor's head. It was a little dangerous, because even a simple question could bring on a half-hour explanation. His grandma had always said, "Ask your daddy the time, and he tells you how to make a clock." But he was so happy explaining, and Gregor was just happy being with him. Besides, Gregor had loved the rain forest exhibit, and the cafeteria with french fries shaped like dinosaurs. They had never really figured out how the fish had known to grow eyes. His dad had had some theories, of course, but he couldn't explain how the fish had been able to change so fast.

Gregor wondered how long it took people to become transparent with purple eyes. He turned to Vikus. "So, you were going to tell me how you got down here?"

While Gregor tried not to wolf his food, which turned out to be delicious, Vikus filled him in on the history of Regalia.

Not all of it was clear, but it seemed the people had come from England in the 1600s. "Yes, they were led here by a stonemason, one Bartholomew of Sandwich," said Vikus, and Gregor had to work to keep a straight face. "He had visions of the future. He saw the Underland in a dream, and he set out to find it."

Sandwich and a group of followers had sailed to New York, where he got on famously with the local tribe. The Underland was no secret to the Native Americans, who had made periodic trips below the earth for ritual purposes for hundreds of years. They had little interest in living there and didn't care if Sandwich was mad enough to want to.

"Of course, he was quite sane," said Vikus. "He knew that one day the earth would be empty of life except what was sustained beneath the ground."

Gregor thought it might be rude to tell Vikus that billions of people lived up there now. Instead, he asked, "So, everybody just packed up and moved down here?"

"Heavens, no! It was fifty years before the eight hundred were down and the gates to the Overland sealed. We had to know we could feed ourselves and have walls to keep us safe. Rome was not built in a day." Vikus laughed. "This was how Fred Clark the Overlander said it."

"What happened to him?" asked Gregor, spearing a mushroom. The table got quiet.

"He died," said Solovet softly. "He died without your sun."

Gregor lowered the mushroom to his plate. He looked over at Boots, who was covered from head to toe in some kind of mushy baby stew. She sleepily finger-painted on the stone tabletop with the gravy.

"Our sun," thought Gregor. Had it set? Was it bedtime? Had the police gone, or were they still there questioning his mom? If they'd gone, he knew where she'd be. Sitting at the kitchen table. Alone in the dark. Crying.

Suddenly he couldn't stand to hear another word about the Underland. He just had to get out of it.

CHAPTER

7

The darkness pressed down on Gregor's eyes until he felt it had physical weight, like water. He'd never been completely without light before. At home, streetlights, car headlights, and the occasional flashing fire truck shone in the tiny window of his bedroom. Here, once he'd blown out the oil lamp, it was as if he'd lost the sense of sight entirely.

He'd been tempted to relight the lamp. Mareth had told him that torches burned all night long in the corridor outside his room and he could rekindle the flame there. But he wanted to save the oil. He'd be lost without it once he got out of Regalia.

Boots made a snuffling sound and pressed her back deeper into his side. His arm tightened around her. Servants had prepared separate beds for them, but Boots had climbed right in with Gregor.

It hadn't been hard to get the Underlanders to excuse them for bed. Everyone could see Boots could barely keep her eyes open, and he must have looked pretty ragged himself. He wasn't. Adrenaline was pumping through him so fast, he was afraid that people could hear his heart beating through the heavy curtains that shut off their bedroom from the hall. The last thing he could do was sleep.

They had been invited to bathe again before bed. It was something of a necessity for Boots, who, in addition to stew, had conditioned her curls with some kind of pudding. Gregor hadn't objected, either. The water gave him a quiet place to think out his escape plan.

It also gave him a chance to ask Dulcet about the water system in the palace without seeming suspicious. "How do you guys have hot and cold running water?" he asked.

She told him the water was pumped from a series of hot and cold springs.

"And then it just empties back into a spring?" he asked innocently.

"Oh, no, that would not be fresh," said Dulcet. "The dirty water falls into the river beneath the palace and then flows to the Waterway."

It was just the information he needed. The river beneath the palace was their way out. Even better, it led to the Waterway. He didn't know what that was exactly, but Vikus had mentioned it had two gateways to the Overland.

Boots stirred again in her sleep, and Gregor patted her side to quiet her. She had not seemed to miss home until bedtime. But she looked worried when he told her it was time to go to sleep.

"Mama?" she asked. "Liz-ee?"

Was it only that morning that Lizzie had ridden off to camp on the bus? It seemed like a thousand years ago.

"Home? Mama?" insisted Boots. Even though she was exhausted, he had a hard time getting her to sleep. Now he could tell by how restless she was that she was having vivid dreams.

"Probably full of giant cockroaches and bats," he thought.

He had no way to tell how much time had passed. An hour? Two? But what little noise he'd been able to hear through the curtain had ceased. If he was going to do this thing, he needed to get started.

Gregor gently disengaged himself from Boots and stood up. He fumbled in the dark and found the sling Dulcet had given him. Trying to position Boots inside it proved tricky. Finally he just squeezed his eyes shut and let his other senses work. That was easier. He slid her in and slung the pack on his back.

Boots murmured, "Mama," and her head fell against his shoulder.

"I'm working on it, baby," he whispered back, and searched the table for the lamp. That was all he was taking. Boots, the pack, and the lamp. He'd need his hands for other things.

Gregor groped his way to the curtain and pushed the edge aside. There was enough torchlight from the far hall for him to make out the passage was empty. The

Underlanders had not bothered to post guards at his door now that they knew him better. They were making an effort to make him feel like a guest and, anyway, where would he go?

"Down the river," he thought grimly. "Wherever that leads."

He crept along the hall taking care to place each of his bare feet silently. Thankfully Boots slept on. His plan would disintegrate if she woke before he got out of the palace.

Their bedroom was conveniently close to the bathroom, and Gregor followed his way to the watery sound. His plan was simple. The river ran under the palace. If he could make his way to the ground floor without losing the sound of water, he should find the place it drained into the river.

If the plan was simple, its execution was not. It took Gregor several hours to weave his way down through the palace. The bathrooms were not always near the stairs, and he found himself having to backtrack so he wouldn't lose the sound of rushing water. Twice he had to duck into rooms and hide when he spotted Underlanders. There weren't many about, but some sort of guards patrolled the palace at night.

Finally the sound of water became stronger, and he made his way to the lowest level of the building. He followed his ears to where the roar was loudest and sneaked through a doorway.

For a moment, Gregor almost abandoned his plan. When Dulcet had said "river," he had pictured the rivers that flowed through New York City. But this Underland river looked like something out of an action adventure movie. It wasn't terribly wide, but it ran with such speed that the surface was churned into white foam. He couldn't guess its depth, but it had enough power to carry large boulders by as if they were empty soda cans. No wonder the Underlanders didn't bother to post a guard on the dock. The river was more dangerous than any army they could assemble.

"But you must be able to travel on it — they have boats," thought Gregor, noticing half a dozen crafts tied up above the rush of the current. They were made out of some kind of skin stretched over a frame. They reminded him of the canoes at camp.

Camp! Why couldn't he just be at camp like a normal kid?

Trying not to think of the bobbing boulders, he lit his oil lamp from a torch by the dock. On reflection, he took the torch as well. Where he was going, light would be as important as air. He blew out the oil lamp to save fuel.

He carefully climbed into one of the boats and checked it out. The torch slid into a holder clearly designed for it.

"How do you get this thing down in the water?" he wondered. Two ropes held it aloft. They were attached to a metal wheel that was affixed to the dock. "Well, here goes nothing," Gregor said, and gave the wheel a yank. It gave a loud creak, and the boat fell straight into the river, knocking Gregor on his rear end.

The current swept up the boat like it was a dried leaf. Gregor grasped the sides and hung on as they shot into the darkness. Hearing voices, he managed to look back at the dock for a moment. Two Underlanders were screaming something after him. The river curved and they vanished from sight.

Would they come after him? Of course they would come after him. But he had a head start. How far was it to the Waterway? *What* was the Waterway, and once he got there, where did he go next?

Gregor would have been more concerned about these questions if he wasn't trying so hard to stay alive. Along with the boulders, he had to dodge the jagged black rocks that jutted out of the water. He found an oar lying along the bottom of the boat and used it to deflect the canoe off the rocks.

The temperature of the Underland had felt com-fortably cool since he'd arrived, especially after the ninety-degree heat of his apartment. But the cold wind whipping up off the water made goose bumps rise on his flesh.

"Gregor!" He thought he'd heard someone call his name.

Was it his imagination or — no! There it was again. The Underlanders must be closing in on him.

The river swerved and suddenly he could see a little better. A long cavern lined with crystals shimmered around him, reflecting back his torchlight.

Gregor made out a glittering beach flanking one side of the river up ahead. A tunnel led from the beach into the dark. On impulse, Gregor pushed off a rock and pointed the canoe toward the beach. He paddled desperately with the oar for the shore. Staying on the river was no use. The Underlanders were breathing down his neck. Maybe he had time to pull up on the beach and hide in the tunnel. After they'd passed by, he could wait a few hours and try the river again.

The canoe slammed into the beach. Gregor caught himself just before his face hit the boat bottom. Boots jerked partly awake and cried a little, but he soothed her back to sleep with his voice as he struggled to pull his craft across the sand with one hand while carrying the torch with the other. "It's okay, Boots. Shhh. Go back to sleep."

"Hi, Bat," she murmured and her head plopped back on his shoulder.

Gregor heard his name in the distance and sped up. He had just reached the mouth of the tunnel when he ran headfirst into something warm and furry. Startled, he staggered back a few paces, dropping the torch. The something stepped out into the dim light. Gregor's knees turned to jelly and he sunk slowly to the sand.

The face of a monstrous rat broke into a smile.

CHAPTER

8

"Ah, here you are at last," said the rat idly. "By your reek we expected you ages ago. Look, Fangor, he has brought the pup."

A long nose poked over the first rat's shoulder. It had a friend.

"What a tidbit she is," said Fangor in a smooth, rich voice. "I will allow you the entire boy if I may have the sweetness of the pup to myself, Shed."

"It is tempting, but he is more bone than meat, and she is such a morsel," said Shed. "I find myself quite torn by your offer. Stand you, boy, and let us better tell your stuffing."

The cockroaches had been freaky, the bats intimidating, but these rats were purely terrifying. Sitting back on their haunches, they were a good six feet tall, and their legs, arms, whatever you called them, bulged with muscle under their gray fur. But the worst part of all was their teeth, six-inch incisors that protruded out of their whiskered mouths.

No, the worst part was that they were clearly planning to eat Gregor and Boots. Some people thought rats didn't eat people, but Gregor knew better. Even the regular-sized rats back home would attack a person if they were helpless. Rats preyed on babies, old people, the weak, the defenseless. There were stories . . . the homeless man in the alley . . . a little boy who'd lost two fingers . . . they were too horrible to think about.

Gregor slowly got to his feet, retrieving the torch, but keeping it down at his side. He pressed Boots back against the cavern wall.

Fangor's nose quivered. "This one had fish for supper. Mushrooms, grain, and just a bit of leaf. Now that's flavorful, you must admit, Shed."

"But the pup has gorged on stewed cow and cream," returned Shed. "Not to mention, she is clearly milk-fed herself."

Now Gregor knew what all the fuss about bathing had been. If the rats could detect the handful of greens he'd eaten hours earlier, they must have an unbelievable sense of smell.

The Underlanders hadn't been rude when they'd wanted him to bathe. They had been trying to keep him alive!

He went from attempting to evade them to wishing desperately that they'd find him. He had to hold the rats off. It would give him time. The expression startled him.

Vikus had said killing him would give the roaches no time. By "time," did the Underlanders simply mean more life?

He brushed off his clothes and tried to adopt the rats' casual banter. "Do I have any say in this?" he asked.

To his surprise, Fangor and Shed laughed. "He speaks!" said Shed. "What a treat! Usually we get nothing but shrieks and whimpers! Tell us, Overlander, what makes you so brave?"

"Oh, I'm not brave," said Gregor. "Bet you can smell that."

The rats laughed again. "True, your sweat carries much fear, but still you have managed to address us."

"Well, I thought you might like to get to know your meal better," said Gregor.

"I like him, Shed!" howled Fangor.

"I like him, too!" choked Shed. "The humans are commonly most dreary. Say we may keep him, Fangor."

"Oh, Shed, how is that to be? It would entail much explaining, and besides, all this laughter gives me hunger," said Fangor.

"And me," said Shed. "But you must agree, to eat such amusing prey is a great pity."

"A great pity, Shed," said Fangor. "But without remedy. Shall we?"

And with that, both rats bared their teeth and moved in on him. Gregor slashed at them with the torch sending a trail of sparks through the air. He held it in front of him with both hands, like a sword, fully illuminating his face.

The rats pulled up short. At first he thought they were afraid of the flame, but it was something more. They looked stunned.

"Mark you, Shed, his shade," said Fangor in a hushed voice.

"I mark it, Fangor," said Shed quietly. "And he is but a boy. Think you he is . . . ?"

"He is not if we kill him!" Fangor growled, and lunged for Gregor's throat.

The first bat came in so silently that neither Gregor nor the preoccupied rats saw it. It caught Fangor mid-leap, knocking him off course.

Fangor plowed into Shed, and the rats landed in a heap. Instantly they regained their feet and turned on their assailants.

Gregor saw Henry, Mareth, and Perdita zigzagging their bats above the rats' heads. Besides avoiding one another in limited space, they had to dodge the wicked claws of the rats. Fangor and Shed could easily leap ten feet in the air, and the sparkling ceiling of the cavern over the beach was not much higher.

The humans began to dive at the rats, wielding swords. Fangor and Shed fought back viciously with claws and teeth. Blood began to stain the beach, but Gregor couldn't tell whose it was.

"Flee!" Henry shouted at Gregor as he whipped past him. "Flee, Overlander!"

Part of him wanted to, badly, but he couldn't. First of all, he had no idea where to go. His boat was high on the beach, and the tunnel . . . well, he'd rather take his chances in the open than in the tunnel if he had to deal with the rats.

More important, he knew the Underlanders were only here because of him. He couldn't just run away and leave them to face the rats.

But what could he do?

At that moment, Shed caught the wing of Mareth's bat in his teeth and hung on. The bat struggled to free itself, but Shed held fast. Perdita came in behind Shed, taking off his ear with one stroke of her sword. Shed gave a howl of pain, releasing Mareth's bat.

But as Perdita pulled out of her dive, Fangor leaped onto her bat, ripping a chunk of fur off its throat and hurling her to the ground. Perdita hit her head on the cavern wall as she landed and was knocked out. Fangor loomed over her and aimed his teeth at her neck.

Gregor didn't remember thinking of his next move, it just happened. One minute he was pressed against the wall, and the next he had jumped forward and thrust his torch into Fangor's face. The rat shrieked and stumbled backward, right into Henry's sword. Fangor's lifeless body fell to the ground, taking the sword with it.

Fangor's shriek finally woke Boots, who took one look over Gregor's shoulder and began wailing at the top of her lungs. Her cries echoed off the walls, sending Shed into a frenzy and disorienting the bats.

"How fly you, Mareth?" yelled Henry.

"We can hold!" cried Mareth, although his bat was spraying blood from its wounded wing.

Things didn't look good. Mareth's bat was losing control, Henry was unarmed, Perdita was unconscious, her bat was gasping for air on the ground, Boots was screeching, and Shed was insane with pain and fear. Though bleeding badly, he had lost none of his speed or strength.

Mareth was trying desperately to keep the rat from Perdita, but he was just one guy. Henry flew interference, but he couldn't get in too close without a sword. Gregor crouched over Perdita holding the torch. It seemed a fragile defense against the crazed Shed, but he had to do something.

Then Shed leaped, catching Mareth's bat by the feet. The bat slammed into the wall and so did Mareth. The rat turned on Gregor.

"Now you die!" screamed Shed. Boots screamed back in terror as Shed lunged at them. Gregor braced himself, but Shed never made it. Instead, the rat let out a gasp and pawed at the blade that jutted through its throat.

Gregor caught a glimpse of Luxa's bat, Aurora, flipping upright. He had no idea when she'd arrived. Luxa must have been flying completely upside down when she'd stabbed Shed. Even though Luxa had flattened herself on the bat's back, Aurora barely managed to pull out of the maneuver without scraping her off on the ceiling.

Shed slumped back against the cavern wall, but there was no fight left in him. His eyes burned into Gregor's. "Overlander," he gurgled, "we hunt you to the last rat." And with that, he died.

Gregor had only a moment to catch his breath before Henry landed beside him. Pushing Gregor out onto the beach, he lifted Perdita in his arms and took off, yelling, "Scorch the land!"

Blood pouring down his face from a gash on his forehead, Mareth was already wrenching the swords from Shed and Fangor. He dragged the rats into the river, and it quickly carried their bodies away. His bat shakily regained the use of its wings and he hurdled onto its back. Mareth caught Boots's backpack and hoisted Gregor onto his stomach in front of him.

Gregor saw Aurora hook her clawed feet into the fur at the shoulders of Perdita's injured bat. Luxa had at some point retrieved the oil lamp from the boat. As they rose into the air, she smashed it onto the ground.

"Drop the torch!" yelled Mareth, and Gregor managed to straighten his fingers, releasing it.

The last thing he saw as they darted out of the cavern was the beach bursting into flame.

CHAPTER

Gregor watched the water flash under his eyes as he clung to the bat. For a moment, he felt relieved to have escaped the rats. But the fear of hurtling through the air on a wounded bat quickly overcame him.

Boots had her arms clasped so tightly around his neck that he could barely breathe, let alone speak. And what would he say to Mareth, anyway? "Wow, I'm really sorry about that whole thing back on the beach?"

He'd had no idea, of course, about the rats. But hadn't the Underlanders tried to warn him? No, they had spoken of danger, but no one had specifically mentioned rats except the cockroaches. "Rat bad," one had said. And later they had talked about how much the rats would pay to bargain with Luxa. He and Boots could have been sold to the rats, and then what?

He felt nauseous and shut his eyes to block out the churning water. The image of the carnage on the beach filled his head, and he decided the view of the water was better. It turned to blackness as the light from the fire diminished. When light flickered off the waves again he knew they were nearing Regalia.

A group of Underlanders waited on the dock. They whisked the unconscious Perdita and her bleeding bat away. They tried to take Mareth on a stretcher, but he brushed them off and insisted on helping to carry his bat inside.

Gregor sat on the dock, where Mareth had shoved him as they'd landed, wishing he could disappear. Boots was quiet now, but he could feel her little muscles were rigid with fear. Fifteen, twenty minutes passed, maybe. He couldn't tell.

"Up!" someone snarled at him, and he saw Mareth glaring down at him. The gash on his forehead was bandaged, the right side of his face bruised and swollen. "Find your feet, Overlander!" Mareth barked. Had he actually thought this guy was shy a few hours ago?

Gregor slowly straightened his stiff legs and stood. Mareth tightly tied his hands behind his back. No question about it this time: He was definitely a prisoner. Another guard joined Mareth, and they marched Gregor ahead of them. His legs moved numbly. What would they do to him now?

He paid no attention to where they were going. He just walked whatever way he was pushed. He had a vague sense of climbing a lot of stairs before he entered a large diamond-shaped room. There was a table in the middle of it. Mareth pushed him down on a stool by a roaring fireplace. The two guards stepped back a couple of paces, watching him like hawks.

"I'm that dangerous," he thought foggily.

Boots began to stir on his back. She tugged on one of his ears. "Home?" she pleaded. "Go home, Ge-go?" Gregor had no answer for her.

People were hurrying past the door, talking in excited voices. Some peered in at him, but no one came in.

In the warmth of the fire, he realized he was frozen. He was soaked in river water up to his waist and shivering from the wind and the horror of what he'd witnessed. Of what he'd taken part in.

Boots was in better condition. Her backpack seemed to be waterproof, and she was pressed up against him. Still, her toes felt like ice when they brushed his arm.

Fatigue washed over Gregor, and he wished he could lie down, just lie down and fall asleep and wake up in his bed where he could see the car lights flashing across the walls. But he had given up thinking this was a dream.

What had happened to the Underlanders? Perdita? Her wounded bat? And Mareth's? If they died, it would be his fault. He wouldn't even try to argue that.

Just then Luxa appeared. Burning white with fury, she crossed the room and struck him on the face. His head snapped to the side and Boots let out a cry.

"No hitting!" she squeaked. "No, no, no hitting!" She shook her tiny index finger at Luxa. Hitting was absolutely forbidden in Gregor's house, and it had only taken Boots a few time-outs to realize it.

Apparently it wasn't acceptable among the Underlanders, either, because Gregor heard Vikus's voice ring out sharply from the doorway. "Luxa!"

Looking like she'd love to slap him again, Luxa stalked to the mantel and glared into the fire.

"For shame, Luxa," Vikus said, crossing to her.

She turned on him, spitting venom. "Two fliers are down, and we cannot awaken Perdita because the Overlander must escape! Strike him? I say we throw him into the Dead Land and let him take his chances!" shouted Luxa.

"Be that as it may, Luxa, this is not seemly," said Vikus, but Gregor could see the news had upset him. "Both rats are dead?" he asked.

"Dead and in the river," said Luxa. "We scorched the land."

"This matter of 'we' you and I shall take up later," said Vikus severely. "The council is not pleased."

"I care not what pleases the council," muttered Luxa, but she avoided Vikus's gaze.

"So she wasn't supposed to be there," thought Gregor. "She's in trouble, too." He wished he could enjoy the moment, but he was too wracked with worry, guilt, and exhaustion to care. Besides, Luxa had saved his life taking out Shed. He owed her one, he guessed, but he was still stinging from the slap, so he didn't bring it up.

"No hitting," said Boots again, and Vikus turned to them.

Like Luxa, Gregor was unable to meet his eyes. "What did the Overlander, Luxa? Fight or flee?" asked Vikus.

"Henry says he fought," Luxa admitted grudgingly. "But without skill or knowledge of weapons."

Gregor felt like saying, "Hey, all I had was a stupid torch!" But why bother?

"Then he has much courage," said Vikus.

"Courage without caution makes for early death, or so you tell me daily," said Luxa.

"So I tell you and do you hear?" said Vikus, raising his eyebrows. "You hear not as he hears not. You are both very young for deafness. Unleash his hands and leave us," he said to the guards.

Gregor felt a blade cut through the ropes on his wrists. He rubbed the marks trying to restore circulation to his hands. His cheek throbbed, but he wouldn't give Luxa the satisfaction of seeing him touch it.

Boots reached over his shoulder and touched the creases on his wrists. "Ow," she whimpered. "Ow."

"I'm okay, Boots," he said, but she just shook her head.

"Gather us here," said Vikus, sitting at the table. Neither Gregor nor Luxa moved. "Gather us here, for we must discuss!" said Vikus, slapping his hand on the stone surface. This time, they both took seats as far from each other as possible.

Gregor pulled Boots up over his head and out of the backpack. She settled on his lap, wrapping Gregor's arms tightly around her and looking at Vikus and Luxa with large, solemn eyes.

75

"I guess after tonight Boots won't think the whole world is her friend," thought Gregor. She had to find out sometime, but it still made him sad.

Vikus began, "Gregor the Overlander, there is much you do not understand. You do not speak, but your face speaks for you. You are worried. You arc angered. You believe you were right to flee those who kept you against your will, but feel sorely that we have suffered in your saving. We told you not of the rats, yet Luxa blames you for our losses. We seem to be your enemy, and yet we gave you time."

Gregor didn't answer. He thought that pretty much summed things up except for the fact that Luxa had hit him.

Vikus read his mind. "Luxa should not have struck you, but your fight invited horrible death to those she loved. This is greatly felt by her, as both her parents were killed by rats."

Luxa gasped. "That is not his affair!"

She looked so distressed that Gregor almost objected as well. Whatever she'd done to him, this wasn't his business.

"But I make it so, Luxa, as I have cause to believe that Gregor may himself lack a father," continued Vikus.

Now it was Gregor's turn to look shocked. "How do you know that?"

"I do not know for sure, I only guess. Tell me, Gregor the Overlander, recognize you this?" Vikus reached in his cloak and pulled something out.

It was a metal ring. Several keys dangled from it. But it was the roughly braided loop of red, black, and blue leather that made Gregor's heart stop. He had woven it himself during crafts class at the very same summer camp that Lizzie was at now. You could make three things: a bracelet, a bookmark, or a key chain. Gregor had picked the key chain.

His father never went anywhere without it.

PART 2

THE QUEST

CHAPTER

10

When Gregor's heart started up again, it beat so hard, he thought it might break through his chest. His hand reached out on its own, his fingers grasping for the key chain. "Where'd you get that?"

"I told you other Overlanders have fallen. Some years ago we rescued one very like you in face and feature. I cannot recall the exact date," said Vikus, placing the key chain in Gregor's hand.

"Two years, seven months, and thirteen days ago," thought Gregor. Aloud, he said, "It belongs to my dad."

Waves of happiness washed over him as he ran his fingers over the worn leather braid and the metal snap that allowed you to attach it to your belt loop. Memories flashed through his mind. His dad fanning out the keys to find the one to open the front door. His dad jingling the keys in front of

Lizzie in her stroller. His dad on a picnic blanket in Central Park, using a key to pry open a container of potato salad.

"Your father?" Luxa's eyes widened, and a strange expression crossed her face. "Vikus, you do not think he —"

"I do not know, Luxa. But the signs are strong," said Vikus. "My mind has been on little else since he arrived."

Luxa turned to Gregor, her violet eyes quizzical.

What? What was her problem now?

"Your father, like you, was desperate to return home. With much difficulty we persuaded him to stay some weeks, but the strain proved too great and one night, also like you, he slipped away," said Vikus. "The rats reached him before we did."

Gregor smashed into reality, and the joy drained out of him. Of course, there were no other living Overlanders in Regalia. Vikus had told him that in the stadium. His dad had tried to get home and had met up with the same fate Gregor had. Only the Underlanders hadn't been there to save him. He swallowed the lump in his throat. "He's dead then."

"So we assumed. But then came rumor the rats had kept him living," said Vikus. "Our spies confirm this regularly."

"He's alive?" asked Gregor, feeling hope rush back through him. "But why? Why didn't they kill him?"

"We know not why with certainty, but I have suspicions. Your father was a man of science, was he not?" asked Vikus.

"Yeah, he teaches science," said Gregor. He couldn't make sense of what Vikus was saying. Did the rats want his dad to teach chemistry?

"In our conversations, it was clear he understood the workings of nature," said Vikus. "Of trapped lightning, of fire, of powders that explode."

Gregor was beginning to catch his drift. "Look, if you think my dad's making guns or bombs for the rats, you can forget it. He would never do that."

"It is hard to imagine what any of us would do in the caves of the rats," said Vikus gently. "To keep sanity must be a struggle, to keep honor a Herculean feat. I am not judging your father, only seeking to explain why he survives so long."

"The rats fight well in close range. But if we attack from afar, they have no recourse but to run. Of all things, they wish a way to kill us at a distance," said Luxa. She didn't seem to be accusing his father, either. And she didn't seem mad at him anymore. Gregor wished she'd stop staring at him.

"My wife, Solovet, has a different theory," said Vikus, brightening a little. "She believes the rats want your father to make them a thumb!"

"A thumb?" asked Gregor. Boots held up her thumb to show him. "Yeah, little girl, I know what a thumb is," he said, smiling down at her.

"Rats have no thumbs and therefore cannot do many things that we can. They cannot make tools or weapons. They are masters of destruction, but creation evades them," said Vikus.

"Be glad, Overlander, if they believe your father can be useful. It is all that will give him time," said Luxa sadly.

"Did you meet my dad, too?" he asked.

"No," she replied. "I was too young for such meetings."

"Luxa was still concerned with her dolls then," said Vikus. Gregor tried hard to imagine Luxa with a doll and couldn't.

"My parents met him, and spoke him well," said Luxa.

Her parents. She'd still had parents then. Gregor wondered about how the rats had killed them, but knew he'd never ask.

"Luxa speaks true. At present, the rats are our bitter enemies. If you meet a rat outside the walls of Regalia, you have two choices: to fight or be killed. Only the hope of a great advantage would keep a human alive in their paws. Especially an Overlander," said Vikus.

"I don't see why they hate us so much," said Gregor. He thought of Shed's burning eyes, his last words, "Overlander, we hunt you to the last rat." Maybe they knew how people in the Overland tried to trap, poison, and kill off all the rats aboveground. Except the ones they used in lab experiments.

Vikus and Luxa exchanged a look. "We must tell him, Luxa. He must know what he faces," said Vikus.

"Do you really think it is he?" she said.

"Who? He, who?" said Gregor. He had a bad feeling about where this conversation was going.

Vikus rose from the table. "Come," he said, and headed out the door.

Gregor got up, willing his stiff arms to carry Boots. He and Luxa reached the door at the same time and stopped. "After you," he said.

She glanced at him sideways and followed Vikus.

The halls were lined with Underlanders who watched them pass in silence and then broke into whispers. They did not have far to go before Vikus stopped at a polished wooden door. Gregor realized it was the first wooden thing he'd seen in the Underland. What had Vikus said about something being "as rare as trees"? For trees, you needed lots of light, so how would they grow here?

Vikus pulled out a key and opened the door. He took a torch from a holder in the hall and led the way in.

Gregor stepped into a room that seemed to be an empty stone cube. On every surface were carvings. Not just the walls but the floor and ceiling, too. These weren't the frolicking animals he'd seen elsewhere in Regalia, these were words. Tiny words that must've taken forever to chisel out.

"A-B-C," said Boots, which is what she always said when she saw letters. "A-B-C-D," she added for emphasis.

"These are the prophecies of Bartholomew of Sandwich," said Vikus. "Once we sealed the gates, he devoted the rest of his life to recording them."

"I bet he did," thought Gregor. It sounded like just the kind of thing crazy old Sandwich would do. Drag a bunch of people underground and then lock himself in a room and chip out more crazy stuff on the walls.

"So, what do you mean, prophecies?" asked Gregor, although he knew what prophecies were. They were predictions of what would happen in the future. Most religions had them, and his grandma loved a book of them by a guy named Nostra-something. To hear her talk, the future was pretty depressing.

"Sandwich was a visionary," said Vikus. "He foretold many things that have happened to our people."

"And a bunch that haven't?" asked Gregor, trying to sound innocent. He hadn't ruled out prophecies entirely, but he was skeptical about anything Sandwich came up with. Besides, even if someone told you something that would happen in the future, what could you do about it?

"Some we have not yet unraveled," admitted Vikus.

"He foretold my parents' end," said Luxa sorrowfully, running her fingers over part of the wall. "There was no mystery in that."

Vikus put his arm around her and looked at the wall. "No," he agreed softly. "That was as clear as water."

Gregor felt awful for about the tenth time that night. From now on, whatever he thought, he would try to talk about the prophecies with respect.

"But there is one that hangs most heavily over our heads. It is called 'The Prophecy of Gray,' for we know not whether it be fair or foul," said Vikus. "We do know that it was to Sandwich the most sacred and maddening of his visions. For he could never see the outcome, although it came to him many times."

Vikus gestured to a small oil lamp that illuminated a panel of the wall. It was the only light in the room besides the torch. Maybe they kept it burning constantly.

"Will you read?" asked Vikus, and Gregor approached the panel. The prophecy was written like a poem, in four parts. Some of the lettering was odd, but he could make it out.

"A-B-C," said Boots, touching the letters. Gregor began to read.

> BEWARE, UNDERLANDERS, TIME HANGS BY A THREAD.
> THE HUNTERS ARE HUNTED, WHITE WATER RUNS RED.
> THE GNAWERS WILL STRIKE TO EXTINGUISH THE REST.
> THE HOPE OF THE HOPELESS RESIDES IN A QUEST.
>
> AN OVERLAND WARRIOR, A SON OF THE SUN,
> MAY BRING US BACK LIGHT, HE MAY BRING US BACK NONE.
> BUT GATHER YOUR NEIGHBORS AND FOLLOW HIS CALL
> OR RATS WILL MOST SURELY DEVOUR US ALL.
>
> TWO OVER, TWO UNDER, OF ROYAL DESCENT,
> TWO FLYERS, TWO CRAWLERS, TWO SPINNERS ASSENT.
> ONE GNAWER BESIDE AND ONE LOST UP AHEAD.
> AND EIGHT WILL BE LEFT WHEN WE COUNT UP THE DEAD.
>
> THE LAST WHO WILL DIE MUST DECIDE WHERE HE STANDS.
> THE FATE OF THE EIGHT IS CONTAINED IN HIS HANDS.
> SO BID HIM TAKE CARE, BID HIM LOOK WHERE HE LEAPS,
> AS LIFE MAY BE DEATH AND DEATH LIFE AGAIN REAPS.

Gregor finished the poem and didn't know quite what to say. He blurted out, "What's that mean?"

Vikus shook his head. "No one knows for certain. It tells of a dark time when the future of our people is undecided.

It calls for a journey, not just of humans but of many creatures, which may lead either to salvation or ruin. The journey will be led by an Overlander."

"Yeah, well, I got that part. This warrior guy," said Gregor.

"You asked why the rats hate Overlanders so deeply. It is because they know one will be the warrior of the prophecy," said Vikus.

"Oh, I see," said Gregor. "So, when's he coming?"

Vikus fixed his eyes on Gregor. "I believe he is already here."

CHAPTER

11

Gregor awoke from a fitful sleep. Images of bloodred rivers, his dad surrounded by rats, and Boots falling into bottomless caverns had woven in and out of his dreams all night long.

Oh, yeah. And then there was that warrior thing.

He had tried to tell them. When Vikus had implied that he was the warrior in "The Prophecy of Gray," Gregor had actually laughed. But the man was serious.

"You've got the wrong guy," Gregor had said. "Really, I promise, I'm not a warrior."

Why pretend and get their hopes up? Samurai warriors, Apache warriors, African warriors, medieval warriors. He'd seen movies. He'd read books. He didn't in any way resemble any warrior. First of all, they were grown up and they usually had a lot of special weaponry. Gregor was eleven and, unless you counted a two-year-old sister as special weaponry, he'd come empty-handed.

Also, Gregor was not into fighting. He'd fight back if someone jumped him at school, but that didn't happen often. He wasn't all that big, but he moved fast and people didn't like to mess with him. Sometimes he'd step in if a bunch of guys were pounding a small kid; he hated seeing that. But he never picked fights, and wasn't fighting what warriors mainly did?

Vikus and Luxa had listened to his protests. He thought he might have convinced Luxa — she didn't have a very high opinion of him, anyway — but Vikus was more persistent.

"How many Overlanders survive the fall to the Underland, do you suppose? I would guess a tenth. And how many survive the rats after that? Perhaps another tenth. So out of a thousand Overlanders, let us say ten survive. How passing strange is it that not only your father but you and your sister came alive to us," said Vikus.

"I guess it's kind of strange," admitted Gregor. "But I don't see why that makes me the warrior."

"You will when you better understand the prophecy," said Vikus. "Each person carries their own destiny. These walls tell of our destiny. And your destiny, Gregor, requires you to play a role in it."

"I don't know about this destiny thing," said Gregor. "I mean, my dad and Boots and I . . . we all have the same laundry room and we landed somewhere pretty close to you, so I'm thinking it's more of a coincidence. I'd like to help, but you guys are probably going to have to wait a little longer for your warrior."

Vikus just smiled and said they would put it before the council in the morning. This morning. Now.

Despite all of his worries, and he had plenty, Gregor couldn't deny a feeling of giddy happiness that shot through him periodically. His dad was alive! Almost instantly another wave of anxiety would rush over him. "Yeah, he's alive but imprisoned by rats!" Still, his grandma always said, "Where there's life, there's hope."

Boy, wouldn't his grandma love it if she knew he was talked about in a prophecy? But, of course, that wasn't him. That was some warrior guy who would hopefully make an appearance really soon and help him get his dad free.

That was his main goal now. How could he rescue his dad?

The curtain pulled open and Gregor squinted at the light. Mareth stood in the doorway. The swelling in his face had gone down, but his bruises were going to be there for a while.

Gregor wondered if the guard was still angry with him, but Mareth sounded calm. "Gregor the Overlander, the council requests your presence," he said. "If you make haste, you may wash and eat first."

"Okay," said Gregor. He started to rise and realized Boots's head was cradled on his arm. He eased himself up without waking her. "What about Boots?"

"She may sleep on," said Mareth. "Dulcet will watch over her."

Gregor bathed quickly and dressed in fresh clothes. Mareth led him to a small room where a meal was laid out, then stood watch at the door. "Hey, Mareth," he said, drawing the guard's attention. "How is everybody? I mean, Perdita and the bats? Are they okay?"

"Perdita has woken finally. The bats will mend," said Mareth evenly.

"Oh, that's great!" said Gregor with relief. After his father's situation, the thing pressing most on him had been the condition of the Underlanders.

He wolfed down bread, butter, and a mushroom omelette. He drank hot tea made of some sort of herb, and energy seemed to pour through him.

"Are you ready to face the council?" asked Mareth, seeing his empty plate.

"All set!" said Gregor, springing up. He felt better than he had since he had reached the Underland. News of his dad, the Underlanders' recovery, sleep, and food had revived him.

The council, a group of a dozen older Underlanders, had gathered at a round table in a room off the High Hall. Gregor saw Vikus and Solovet, who gave him an encouraging smile.

Luxa was also there, looking tired and defiant. Gregor bet she'd been chewed out for joining the rescue party last night. He was sure she hadn't acted one bit sorry.

Vikus introduced the people around the table. They all had funny-sounding names that Gregor immediately forgot. The council began to ask him questions. All kinds of things, like when he was born and did he know how to swim and what he did in the Overland. He couldn't figure out why a lot of the stuff was important. Did it really matter that his favorite color was green? But a couple of Underlanders were scribbling down every word he said like it was golden.

After a while, the council seemed to forget he was there, and they argued among themselves. He caught phrases like "a son of the sun" and "white water runs red" and knew they were talking about the prophecy.

"Excuse me," he finally broke in. "I guess Vikus didn't tell you, but I'm not the warrior. Look, please, what I really need is for you guys to help me bring my dad home."

Everyone at the table stared at him for a moment and then began to talk with greater excitement. Now he kept hearing the words "follow his call."

Finally Vikus rapped on the table for order. "Members of the council, we must decide. Here sits Gregor the Overlander. Who counts him the warrior of 'The Prophecy of Gray'?"

Ten of the twelve raised their hands. Luxa kept her hands on the table. Either she didn't think he was the warrior or she wasn't allowed to vote. Probably both.

"We believe you to be the warrior," said Vikus. "If you call us to help you regain your father, then we answer your call."

They were going to help him! Who cared why?

"Okay, great!" said Gregor. "Whatever it takes! I mean, believe whatever you want. That's fine."

"We must begin the journey with all haste," said Vikus.

"I'm ready!" said Gregor eagerly. "Let me just get Boots and we can go."

"Ah, yes, the baby," said Solovet. And another round of arguments ensued.

"Wait!" shouted Vikus. "This costs much time. Gregor, we do not know that the prophecy includes your sister."

"What?" said Gregor. He couldn't remember the prophecy very well. He had to ask Vikus if he could get in the room and read it again.

"The prophecy mentions twelve beings. Only two are described as Overlanders. You and your father fill that number," said Solovet.

"The prophecy also speaks of one lost. That one may be your father, in which case Boots is the second Overlander. But it may also be a rat," said Vikus. "The journey will be difficult. The prophecy warns that four of the twelve will lose life. It may be wisest to leave Boots here."

From around the table came a general murmur of assent. Gregor's head began to swim.

Leave Boots? Leave her here in Regalia with the Underlanders? He couldn't do that! It wasn't that he thought they'd mistreat her. But she'd be so lonely, and what if he and his dad didn't make it back? She'd never get home. Still, he knew how vicious the rats were. And they would be hunting him. To the last rat.

He didn't know what to do. He looked at the set faces and thought the Underlanders had already decided to split them up.

"Stay together!" Wasn't that what his mom always told

him when he took his sisters out? "Stay together!"

Then he noticed Luxa was avoiding his gaze. She had intertwined her fingers on the stone table before her and was staring at them tensely. "What would you do if it were your sister, Luxa?" he asked. The room got very quiet. He could tell the council didn't want to hear her opinion.

"I have no sister, Overlander," said Luxa.

Gregor felt disappointed. He heard a murmur of approval from some of the council members. Luxa's eyes flashed around the table and she scowled. "But if I did, and I were you," she said passionately, "I would never take my eyes off her!"

He said, "Thank you," but he didn't think she could hear him in the loud round of objections that poured from the council. He raised his voice. "If Boots doesn't go, I don't go!"

The room was in an uproar when a bat veered through the doorway and crashed onto the table, silencing everyone. A ghostly woman slumped over the bat, pressing her hands to her chest to stem the flow of blood. One of the bat's wings folded in, but the other extended at an awkward angle, clearly broken.

"Anchel is dead. Daphne is dead. The rats found Shed, Fangor. King Gorger has launched his armies. They come for us," gasped the woman.

Vikus caught the woman as she collapsed. "How many, Keeda?" he asked.

"Many," she whispered. "Many rats." And she went limp.

CHAPTER

12

"Sound the alarm!" shouted Vikus, and the place exploded in frantic activity. Horns began blowing, people rushed in and out, bats swooped in for orders and disappeared again without taking the time to land.

Everyone ignored Gregor as they shifted into emergency mode. He wanted to ask Vikus what was going on, but the old man stood in the High Hall in a blur of bat wings giving commands.

Gregor went out on the balcony and could see Regalia swarming like a beehive. Many rats were coming. The Underlanders were going into defense mode. Suddenly he realized they were at war.

The terrifying thought — and the height of the balcony — made Gregor light-headed. As he stumbled back inside, a strong hand caught his arm. "Gregor the

Overlander, prepare yourself, for we leave shortly," said Vikus.

"For where? Where are we gong?" asked Gregor.

"To rescue your father," said Vikus.

"Now? We can go with the rats attacking?" said Gregor. "I mean, there's a war starting, right?"

"Not any war. We believe it is the war foretold in 'The Prophecy of Gray.' The one that may bring about the complete annihilation of our people," said Vikus. "Pursuing the quest for your father is our best hope of surviving it," said Vikus.

"I can take Boots, right?" asked Gregor. "I mean, I'm taking her," he corrected himself.

"Yes, Boots shall come," said Vikus.

"What should I do? You said to prepare myself," asked Gregor.

Vikus thought for a second and called Mareth over. "Take him to the museum, let him choose whatever he thinks may aid him on the journey. Ah, here is the delegation from Troy!" said Vikus. He stepped into another storm of wings.

Gregor ran after Mareth, who had sprinted for the door. Three staircases and several halls later they arrived at a large chamber filled with loaded shelves.

"Here is that which has fallen from the Overland. Remember what you choose you must carry," instructed Mareth, thrusting a leather bag with a drawstring into his hands.

The shelves were filled with everything from baseballs

to car tires. Gregor wished he had time to go through the stuff more carefully; some of it must have been hundreds of years old. But time was a luxury he didn't have. He tried to focus.

What could he take that would help on the trip? What did he need most in the Underland? Light!

He found a flashlight in working condition and collected batteries from every electrical thing he could find.

Something else caught his eye. It was a hard hat like construction workers wore. There was a built-in light on the front, so they could see in the inky tunnels beneath New York City. He grabbed the hat and crammed it on his head.

"We must go!" ordered Mareth. "We must get your sister and take flight!"

Gregor turned to follow him and then he saw it. Root beer! An honest-to-goodness, unopened, only slightly dented can of root beer. It looked pretty new. He knew it was an extravagance, that he should only take essentials, but he had to have it. It was his favorite drink, plus it made him think of home. He stuffed the can in his bag.

The nursery was nearby. Gregor ran in and saw Boots sitting happily among three Underlander toddlers having a tea party. For a second, he almost changed his mind and left her there. Wouldn't she be safer here in the palace? But then he remembered the palace would soon be under siege by rats. Gregor knew he couldn't leave her to face that alone. Whatever happened, they would stay together.

Dulcet quickly helped Gregor into a backpack and slid

Boots inside. She fastened a small bundle to the base of the backpack. "Catch cloths," she said. "A few toys and some treats."

"Thanks," said Gregor, grateful someone had thought of the practical side of traveling with Boots.

"Fare you well, sweet Boots," said Dulcet. She kissed the baby's cheek.

"Bye-bye, Dul-cee," said Boots. "See you soon!"

That was what they always parted with at Gregor's house. Don't worry. I'll be back. I'll see you soon.

"Yes, I will see you soon," said Dulcet, but her eyes filled with tears.

"Take care, Dulcet," said Gregor, giving her hand an awkward shake.

"Fly you high, Gregor the Overlander," she said.

In the High Hall, the mission was readying for departure. Several bats had lit on the ground and were being loaded with supplies.

Gregor saw Henry hugging a painfully thin teenage girl good-bye. She was weeping uncontrollably despite his attempts to comfort her.

"The dreams, brother," she sobbed, "they have worsened. Some terrible evil awaits you."

"Do not distress yourself, Nerissa, I have no plans to die," said Henry soothingly.

"There are evils beyond death," said his sister. "Fly you high, Henry. Fly you high." They embraced, and Henry swung up onto his velvety black bat.

Gregor watched nervously as the girl came his way. He

could never think of the right things to say when people cried. But she had pulled herself together by the time she'd reached him. She held out a small roll of paper. "For you, Overlander," she said. "Fly you high." And before he could answer, she had moved away, leaning on the wall for support.

He opened the paper, which wasn't paper but some sort of dried animal skin, and saw that "The Prophecy of Gray" had been carefully written upon it. "That's so weird," thought Gregor. He had been wishing he could read it again to maybe figure more of it out. He had meant to ask Vikus but had forgotten in the rush. "How did she know I wanted this?" he murmured to Boots.

"Nerissa knows many things. She has the gift," said a boy mounting a golden bat beside him. On second glance, Gregor realized it was Luxa, but her hair had been cropped off close to her head.

"What happened to your hair?" asked Gregor, stuffing the prophecy in his pocket.

"Long locks are dangerous in battle," said Luxa carelessly.

"That's too bad, I mean — it looks good short, too," said Gregor quickly.

Luxa burst out laughing. "Gregor the Overlander, think you my beauty is of any matter in such times?"

Gregor's face felt hot with embarrassment. "That's not what I meant."

Luxa just shook her head at Henry, who was grinning back at her. "The Overlander speaks true, cousin, you look like a shorn sheep."

"All the better," said Luxa. "For who would attack a sheep?"

"Baa," said Boots. "Baaaa." And Henry laughed so hard, he almost fell off his bat. "Sheep says baa," Boots said defensively, which set him off again.

Gregor almost laughed, too. For a moment, he had felt as if he were among friends. But these people had a long way to go before he could consider them friends. To cover his slip, he concentrated on finding a comfortable way to carry his leather bag that would leave his hands free. He tied it to the side strap of the pack.

When he glanced up, he found Luxa looking at him curiously. "What wear you on your head, Overlander?" she asked.

"It's a hard hat. With a light," said Gregor. He flicked it on and off to show her. He could tell she was itching to try it, but she didn't want to ask. Gregor quickly weighed his options in his head. True, they weren't friends . . . but it was better to get along with her if he could. He needed her to get his dad. Gregor held out the hat. "Here, check it out."

Luxa tried to appear indifferent, but her fingers worked the light switch eagerly. "How do you keep the light inside without air? Does it not get hot on your head?" she asked.

"It runs on a battery. It's electricity. And there's a layer of plastic between the light and your head. You can try it on if you want," said Gregor.

Without hesitation, Luxa popped the hat on her head. "Vikus has told me of electricity," she said. She shot the beam of light around the room before returning it to Gregor reluctantly. "Here, you must save your fuel."

"You will begin a new fashion," said Henry cheerfully. He grabbed one of the small stone torches off the wall and laid it on top of his head. Flames seemed to be shooting out of his forehead. "What think you, Luxa?" he asked, showing her his profile with exaggerated haughtiness.

"Your hair is alight!" she suddenly gasped and pointed. Henry dropped the torch and beat at his hair as Luxa went into hysterics.

Realizing it was a joke, Henry caught her in a headlock and rubbed her short hair with his knuckles while she laughed helplessly. For a minute, they could have been a couple of kids in the Overland. Just a brother and sister, like Gregor and Lizzie, wrestling around.

Vikus strode across the hall. "You two are in a merry mood, considering we are at war," he said with a frown as he vaulted onto his bat.

"It is only an excess of spirit, Vikus," said Henry, releasing Luxa.

"Save your spirit — you will have need of it where we are going. Ride you with me, Gregor," said Vikus, extending a hand. Gregor swung up behind him on his big gray bat.

Boots kicked his sides with anticipation. "Me ride, too. Me, too," she chirped.

"Mount up!" called Vikus, and Henry and Luxa leaped onto their bats. Gregor could spot Solovet and Mareth preparing to leave also. Mareth was riding a bat he hadn't seen before. Probably his other bat was still recovering.

"To the air!" ordered Solovet, and the five bats lifted off in a V formation.

As they rose up in the air, Gregor felt like he would burst from excitement and happiness. They were going to get his dad! They would rescue him and take him home and his mother would smile, really smile, again, and there would be holidays to celebrate, not to dread, and music and — and he was getting ahead of himself. He was breaking his rule right and left and in a minute he would stop but for that minute he would go ahead and imagine as much as he wanted.

As they veered sideways over the city of Regalia, Gregor was reminded of the gravity of their task by the manic activity below. The gates to the stadium were being fortified with huge stone slabs. Wagons of food clogged the roads. People carrying children and bundles were hurrying toward the palace. Extra torches were being lit in all quarters, so the city looked almost bathed in sunlight.

"Wouldn't you want it darker if there's going to be an attack?" asked Gregor.

"No, but the rats would. We need our eyes to fight, they do not," said Vikus. "Most of the creatures in the Underland, the crawlers, the bats, the fish, they have no need of light. We humans are lost without it."

Gregor tucked that bit of information away in his brain. The flashlight had been the best thing to bring after all.

The city quickly gave way to farmland, and Gregor had his first glimpse of how the Underlanders fed themselves.

Great fields of some kind of grain grew under row upon row of hanging white lamps.

"What runs the lamps?" asked Gregor.

"They burn with gas from the earth. Your father was most impressed with our fields. He suggested a plan for lighting our city, too, but at the moment, all light must go for food," said Vikus.

"Did an Overlander show you how to do that?" asked Gregor.

"Gregor, we did not leave our minds in the Overland when we fell. We have inventors just as you do, and light is most precious to us. Think you we poor Underlanders might not have stumbled upon some manner of harnessing it ourselves?" said Vikus good-naturedly.

Gregor felt sheepish. He had sort of thought of the Underlanders as backward. They still used swords and wore funny clothes. But they weren't stupid. His dad said even the cavemen had geniuses among them. Somebody had thought up the wheel.

Solovet flew parallel to them, but she was deep in conversation with a pair of bats that had joined the party. She uncurled a large map on her bat's back and scrutinized it.

"Is she trying to find where my dad is?" Gregor asked Vikus.

"She is forming a plan of attack," said Vikus. "My wife leads our warriors. She goes with us not to direct the quest but to gauge the level of support we may expect from our allies."

"Really? I thought you were in charge. Well, you and Luxa," he said, because really, he couldn't tell how that all worked out. Luxa seemed able to order people around, but she could still get in trouble for stuff.

"Luxa will ascend the throne when she turns sixteen. Until then Regalia is ruled by the council. I am but a humble diplomat who spends his spare time trying to teach prudence to the royal youth. You see how well I succeed," Vikus said wryly. He glanced at Henry and Luxa, who were flipping wildly in the sky trying to knock each other off their bats. "Do not let Solovet's gentle demeanor fool you. In the planning of battles, she is more cunning and wily than a rat."

"Wow," said Gregor. Her gentle demeanor *had* fooled him.

Gregor shifted his weight on the bat and something poked his leg. He pulled the prophecy Nerissa had given him from his pocket and unrolled it. Maybe now would be a good time to ask Vikus some questions. "So, do you think you could explain this 'Gray Prophecy' to me?"

"'The Prophecy of Gray,'" corrected Vikus. "What of it puzzles you?"

"The whole thing," thought Gregor, but he said, "Maybe we could just go through it a piece at a time." He studied the poem.

BEWARE, UNDERLANDERS, TIME HANGS BY A THREAD.

Well, that seemed pretty clear. It was a warning.

THE HUNTERS ARE HUNTED, WHITE WATER RUNS RED.

He asked Vikus to unravel the second line. "The rats are traditionally the hunters of the Underland, for they would happily track and kill the rest of us. Last night, we hunted them to save you. So, the hunters were hunted. White water ran red when we left their bodies to the river."

"Oh," said Gregor. Something was bothering him, but he couldn't put his finger on it.

THE GNAWERS WILL STRIKE TO EXTINGUISH THE REST.

"Are 'the gnawers' the rats?" he asked.

"Exactly so," said Vikus.

THE HOPE OF THE HOPELESS RESIDES IN A QUEST.

The quest to get his dad. So, he'd escaped, the Underlanders had saved him, and now they were at war and off on the quest. Gregor suddenly knew what was bothering him. "So . . . this whole thing is my fault!" he said. "It never would've happened if I hadn't tried to escape!" He thought of the approaching army of rats. What had he done?

"No, Gregor, put that from your mind," said Vikus firmly. "You are but one player in a very long and difficult tale. 'The Prophecy of Gray' trapped you, as it trapped us, long ago."

Gregor was silent. He didn't exactly feel better.

"Read on," said Vikus, and Gregor's head drooped to the

page. The lights of Regalia had faded away, and he had to squint to read by the faint torchlight.

> *An Overland warrior, a son of the sun,*
> *May bring us back light, he may bring us back none.*
> *But gather your neighbors and follow his call*
> *Or rats will most surely devour us all.*

"So, you say this next part is about me," he said unhappily.

"Yes, you are the 'Overland warrior,' for obvious reasons," said Vikus, although Gregor didn't think the reasons were too obvious. "You are 'a son of the sun' as an Overlander, but also the son who seeks his father. This is the sort of comedic wordplay Sandwich delighted in."

"Yeah, he was a funny guy," said Gregor glumly. Ha ha.

"Now the lines that follow are most gray," said Vikus. "Sandwich could never clearly see if in fact you succeed in bringing back light or if you fail. But he most adamantly insisted we attempt the venture or die by the rats' teeth."

"Well, that's not too inspiring," said Gregor. But for the first time Sandwich had struck a chord with him. The possibility that Gregor might fail made the whole prophecy more plausible.

"What sort of light am I supposed to bring back?" asked Gregor. "Is there a sacred torch or something?"

"That is a metaphor. By 'light,' Sandwich means 'life.' If the rats can truly extinguish our light, they extinguish our life as well," said Vikus.

A metaphor? Gregor thought an actual torch would be

easier to bring back. How could he bring back some metaphor thing he didn't really understand? "That could be tricky," he said. He read on.

Two over, two under, of royal descent,
Two fliers, two crawlers, two spinners assent.

"What are all those twos about?" asked Gregor.

"That tells us whom we must persuade to accompany us on the quest. We are proceeding as if the 'two over' are you and your sister. 'Two under' of royal descent are Luxa and Henry. Henry's sister, Nerissa, as you might have gleaned, was not a possible choice. Fliers are bats. Crawlers are cockroaches. Spinners are spiders. We go now to assemble our neighbors in the order that the prophecy dictates. First the bats."

The number of bats had been increasing as they flew. Henry led the party into a vast cave. Gregor gave a little jump when he realized the ceiling was bumpy with hundreds and hundreds of hanging bats.

"But don't we already have bats?" asked Gregor.

"We need official permission to take them on the quest," said Vikus. "Also, there are matters of war to discuss."

A towering cylinder of stone sat in the center of the cave. Its sides were as slick as those of the palace. On the round, flat top a group of bats waited.

Vikus turned back to Gregor and whispered, "We humans know you to be the warrior, but other creatures may have doubts. Whoever you think you may or may not be, it is essential that our neighbors believe you are the one."

Gregor was trying to unwind that in his head when they landed next to the bats on the huge pillar of stone. The humans all dismounted. Deep bows and greetings followed on both sides.

One particularly impressive, silvery white bat appeared to be in charge. "Queen Athena," Vikus said, and presented him. "Meet you Gregor the Overlander."

"Be you the warrior? Be you he who calls?" asked the bat in a soft purr.

"Well, actually I —" Gregor saw Vikus frown and pulled up short. He'd been about to go into his spiel about how he wasn't the warrior, but then what? Vikus had whispered something about others believing he was the one. There was a war beginning. The bats weren't likely to send off valuable fliers on a wild-goose chase. If he denied he was the warrior now, the quest would be called off, and his father would be as good as dead. That sealed it.

Gregor stood up straight and tried to control the quaver that slipped into his voice. "I am the warrior. I am he who calls."

The bat was still for a moment, then nodded. "It is he." She spoke with such certainty that for a second Gregor succeeded in thinking of himself as a warrior. A bold, brave, powerful warrior that the Underlanders would tell stories about for centuries. He could almost see himself leading a squadron of bats into battle, stunning the rats, saving the Underland from —

"Ge-go, I pee!" announced Boots.

And there he stood, a boy in a goofy hard hat with a beat-up flashlight and a bunch of batteries he hadn't even tested to see if they still had juice.

The mighty warrior excused himself and changed a diaper.

CHAPTER

13

Vikus and Solovet arranged to have some sort of private war meeting with the bats.

"Do you need me to go along?" asked Gregor. It was less that he thought he could contribute to the meeting and more that he felt safer when Vikus was around. Being stranded on top of a tall pillar surrounded by hundreds of bats made him a little uncomfortable.

And who would be in charge if anything came up? Luxa? That was no good.

"No, thank you, Gregor. We will be discussing battle position for our forces, not the efforts of the quest. We shall not be absent long," said Vikus.

"No problem," said Gregor, but inside he wasn't so sure.

Before they left, Vikus's big gray bat murmured something in Luxa's ear. She smiled, looked at Gregor, and nodded.

"Probably laughing at me saying I'm a warrior," thought Gregor. But that was not it.

"Euripedes says you're bruising his sides," said Luxa. "He wants me to teach you to ride."

That bothered Gregor. He thought he'd been doing pretty well for a first timer. "What's he mean, I'm bruising his sides?"

"You hold on too strongly with your legs. You must trust the bats. They will not drop you," said Luxa. "It is the first lesson we teach the babies."

"Huh," said Gregor. Luxa had a way of putting him down even when she wasn't trying.

"It is easier for the babies," said Mareth quickly. "Like your sister, they have not yet learned much fear. We have a saying down here. 'Courage only counts when you can count.' Can you count, Boots?" Mareth held his fingers up before Boots, who was busy trying to tug off Gregor's sandal. "One . . . two . . . three!"

Boots grinned and held up her pudgy fingers in imitation. "No, me! One . . . two . . . free . . . four seven ten!" she said, and lifted both hands in the air at her accomplishment.

Henry scooped up Boots and held her at arm's length, the way someone might hold a wet puppy. "Boots has no fear, nor will she when she masters counting. You like to fly, do you not, Boots? Go for a ride on the bat?" he said mischievously.

"I ride!" said Boots, and wiggled to get out of Henry's uncomfortable hold.

"Then ride you!" said Henry, and tossed her right off the side of the pillar.

Gregor gasped as he saw Boots, as if in slow motion, sail out of Henry's hands and into the dark.

"Henry!" said Mareth, in shock. But Luxa was cracking up.

Gregor staggered to the side of the pillar and squinted into the darkness. The faint torchlight provided by the bats illuminated only a few yards. Had Henry really thrown Boots to her death? He couldn't believe it. He couldn't —

A happy squeal came from above his head. "More!"

Boots! But what was she doing up there? Gregor fumbled with his flashlight. The beam was strong and cut a wide swath of light through the blackness.

Twenty bats were wheeling around the cave, playing some kind of game of catch with Boots. One would take her up high and flip over, sending the toddler free-falling to the ground. But long before she reached it, another bat would scoop her up gently, only to rise and flip her off again. Boots was giggling ecstatically. "More! More!" she ordered the bats each time she landed. And each time they dropped her, Gregor's stomach lurched into his throat.

"Stop it!" he snapped at the Underlanders. Henry and Luxa looked surprised. Either no one had ever yelled at these royal brats, or they hadn't seen Gregor lose his temper yet. He grabbed Henry by the front of the shirt. "Bring her in now!" Henry could probably cream him, but he didn't care.

Henry put up his hands in mock surrender. "Take ease, Overlander. She is not in danger," he said, grinning.

"In truth, Gregor, she is safer with the bats than in human hands," said Luxa. "And she is not afraid."

"She's two!" screamed Gregor, wheeling on her. "She's going to think she can jump off anything and be caught!"

"She can!" said Luxa, not seeing the problem.

"Not at home, Luxa! Not in the Overland!" said Gregor. "And I don't plan on staying in this creepy place forever!"

They may not have known exactly what he meant by "creepy," but it was pretty clear it was an insult.

Luxa raised her hand, and a bat coasted by lightly flipping Boots into Gregor's arms. He caught her and squeezed her tightly. The Underlanders were no longer laughing.

"What means this 'creepy'?" said Luxa coolly.

"Never mind," said Gregor. "It's just something we Overlanders say when we see our baby sisters being tossed around by bats. See, for us, that's creepy."

"It was meant to be entertaining," said Henry.

"Oh, yeah. You guys should open a theme park. You'll have a line stretched from here to the surface," said Gregor.

Now they really had no idea what he was saying, but his tone was so sarcastic, they couldn't miss it.

Boots wriggled from his arms and ran toward the edge of the pillar. "More, Ge-go!" she piped.

"No, Boots! No, no! No jump!" said Gregor, catching her just in the nick of time. "See, this is just what I'm talking about!" he said to Luxa.

He stuffed Boots into the pack and heaved her onto his back.

The Underlanders were baffled by his anger and stung by his tone, even if they couldn't understand his words.

"Well, it was not Boots who needed the lessons, anyway," said Luxa. "It was you."

"Oh, abandon the thought, Luxa," Henry sneered. "The Overlander would never give himself to the bats. Why, when he returns home, he may forget he is no longer in our 'creepy' land and jump from his own roof!"

Luxa and Henry gave an unfriendly laugh. Mareth just looked embarrassed. Gregor knew it was a dare, and one part of him itched to take it. Just run and jump into the darkness and leave the rest up to the bats. Another part of him didn't want to play this little game. Luxa and Henry wanted him to leap so they could laugh at him flailing around in the air. He guessed they both hated being ignored, though. So he gave them a look of contempt and walked away.

He could feel Luxa positively steaming behind him.

"I could have you thrown off the side, Overlander, and have no one to answer to!" said Luxa.

"So, do it!" said Gregor, holding out his arms. He knew it was a lie. She'd have Vikus to answer to.

Luxa bit her lip in vexation.

"Oh, let the 'warrior' be, Luxa," said Henry. "He is no good to us dead . . . yet . . . and even the bats may not be able to compensate for his clumsiness. Come, I will race you to the pitch pool." She hesitated for a moment, then ran for the edge. She and Henry launched into the air like a pair of beautiful birds and vanished, presumably on their bats.

Gregor stood there, hands on his hips, hating them. He had forgotten Mareth was behind him.

"You must not take what they say to heart," said Mareth softly. Gregor turned and saw the conflict on Mareth's face. "They were both kinder as children, but when the rats took their parents, they changed."

"The rats killed Henry's parents, too?" said Gregor.

"Some years before Luxa's. Henry's father was the king's younger brother. After the Overlanders, the rats would most like to see the royal family dead," said Mareth. "When they were killed, Nerissa became as frail as glass, Henry as hard as stone."

Gregor nodded. He could never hate people very long because he always ended up finding out something sad about them that he had to factor in. Like this kid at school everybody hated because he was always pushing little kids around and then one day they found out his dad had hit him so much, he was in the hospital. With stuff like that, all Gregor could feel was bad.

When Vikus arrived a few minutes later, Gregor got onto his bat without a word. As they took off, he realized how tightly his legs clutched the bat's sides, and tried to loosen up. Vikus rode with his legs swinging free. Gregor let his legs go and found it was actually easier to stay on. More balanced.

"Now we must visit the crawlers," said Vikus. "Do you wish to continue dissecting the prophecy?"

"Maybe later," Gregor answered. Vikus didn't press it. He probably had plenty on his mind with the war and all.

Something else was eating at Gregor now that he had his temper under control. He knew he hadn't refused to jump off the pillar only to make Luxa and Henry mad. And it wasn't only because they'd laugh at him. No mystery why he'd mentioned theme parks. Roller coasters, bungee jumps, parachute drops — he hated them. He went on them sometimes because everybody would think he was a chicken if he didn't, but they weren't fun. What was fun about feeling the world drop out from under your feet? And those rides at least had seat belts.

Gregor hadn't jumped because deep down he was scared to, and everybody knew it.

CHAPTER

14

They flew through dark tunnels for hours. Gregor felt Boots's little head sink down on his shoulder and he let her go. You couldn't let her nap too long during the day or she'd wake up in the middle of the night wanting to play, but how could he keep her awake when it was dark and she couldn't move? He'd deal with it later.

The gloom brought all Gregor's negative thoughts back. His dad imprisoned by rats, his mom crying, the dangers of taking Boots on this unknown voyage, and his own fear at the pillar.

When he felt the bat coasting down for a landing, he was relieved at the distraction, although he disliked meeting up with Luxa and Henry again. He was sure they would be more smug and patronizing than ever.

They dipped into a cavern that was so low, the bats'

wings brushed both the ceiling and floor. When they landed, Gregor dismounted but couldn't straighten up without bumping his hard hat. The place reminded him of a pancake, round and large and flat. He could see why the cockroaches had chosen it. The bats couldn't fly well, and the humans and rats couldn't fight properly with four-foot-high ceilings.

He roused Boots, who seemed to enjoy her new surroundings. She toddled around, standing on tiptoe to touch the ceiling with her fingers. Everyone else just sat on the ground and waited. The bats hunched over, twitching at what Gregor supposed were sounds he couldn't even hear.

A delegation of roaches appeared and bowed low. The humans got to their knees and bowed back, so Gregor did the same. Not one to stand on ceremony, Boots ran up with her arms extended in greeting. "Bugs! Beeg bugs!" she cried.

A happy murmur ran through the group of roaches. "Be she the princess, be she? Be she the one, Temp, be she?"

Boots singled out one roach in particular and patted it between the antennas. "Hi, you! Go ride? We go ride?"

"Knows me, the princess, knows me?" said the roach in awe, and all the other roaches gave little gasps. Even the humans and bats exchanged looks of surprise.

"We go ride? More ride?" said Boots. "Beeg Bug take Boots ride!" she said, patting him more vigorously on the head.

"Gentle, Boots," said Gregor, hurrying to catch her hand.

He placed it softly on the bug's head. "Be gentle, like with puppy dogs."

"Oh, gen-tle, gen-tle," said Boots, lightly bouncing her palm on the roach. It quivered with joy.

"Knows me, the princess, knows me?" the roach whispered. "Recalls she the ride, does she?"

Gregor peered closely at the roach. "Oh, are you the one who carried her to the stadium?" he asked.

The roach nodded in assent. "I be Temp, I be," he said.

Now Gregor knew what all the fuss was about. To his eyes, Temp looked exactly like the other twenty roaches sitting around. How on Earth could Boots have picked him out of the crowd? Vikus looked at him with raised eyebrows as if asking for an explanation, but Gregor could only shrug in reply. It was pretty weird.

"More ride?" pleaded Boots. Temp fell on his face reverently, and she clambered onto his back.

For a minute, everybody just watched them pattering around the chamber. Then Vikus cleared his throat. "Crawlers, we have grave matters to place before you. Take us to your king, take us?"

The roaches reluctantly tore themselves away from watching Boots and led Vikus and Solovet away.

"Oh, great," thought Gregor. "Here we are again." He felt even less comfortable than when Vikus had left the first time. Who knew what Henry and Luxa might do now? And then there was the matter of the giant roaches. He didn't feel particularly safe in the bugs' land. Just yesterday they had considered trading him and Boots to the rats.

Well, at least there was Mareth, who seemed decent enough. And the bats weren't too bad.

Temp and one other roach named Tick had stayed behind. They completely ignored the rest of the party while they took turns giving the toddler rides.

The five bats gathered together in a clump and fell asleep, exhausted from the day's flight.

Mareth placed the torches together to make a small fire and put on some food to warm. Henry and Luxa sat apart speaking in low voices, which was fine with Gregor. Mareth was the only one he felt like talking to, anyway.

"So, can you tell the crawlers apart, Mareth?" asked Gregor. He dumped all his batteries on the ground to sort out the dead ones while they talked.

"No, it is most rare that your sister can. Among us are few that can make distinctions. Vikus is better than most. But to pick one from so many . . . it is passing strange," said Mareth. "Perhaps it is a gift of the Overlanders?" he suggested.

"No, they look identical to me," said Gregor. Boots was really good at those games where they gave you four pictures that looked alike except one had a tiny difference. Like there were four party hats and one had seven stripes instead of six. And if they were all drinking from paper cups, she always knew whose was whose even if they got mixed up on the table together. Maybe every roach really did look distinctly different to her.

Gregor opened up the flashlight. It took two D-size batteries. He swapped the other batteries in and out,

121

trying to determine which ones still had power. As he worked, he inadvertently flipped the switch on when the flashlight was pointing at Luxa and Henry. They jumped, unaccustomed to sudden bursts of light. He did it a couple more times on purpose, which was childish, but he liked seeing them flinch. "They'd last about five seconds in New York City," he thought. That made him feel a little better.

Of the ten batteries, all but two still had juice. Gregor opened up the compartment on his hat and found it ran on some special rectangular battery. Not having any replacements, he would have to use it sparingly. "Maybe I should save this for last. If I lose the others or they go dead, I'll still have this on my head," he thought. He clicked off the light on the hat.

Gregor put the good batteries back in his pocket and set the other two aside. "These two are duds," he said to Mareth. "They don't work."

"Shall I burn them?" asked Mareth, reaching for the batteries.

Gregor caught his wrist before he could toss them in the flames. "No, they might explode!" He didn't really know what would happen if you put a battery in the fire, but he had a vague memory of his dad saying it was a dangerous thing to do. Out of the corner of his eye he caught Luxa and Henry exchanging uneasy glances. "You could blind yourself," he added, just for effect.

Well, that *might* happen if they exploded.

Mareth nodded and gingerly set the dead batteries back

by Gregor. He rolled them around with his sandal, making Luxa and Henry nervous. But when he saw that Mareth looked nervous, too, he stuck the duds in his pocket.

Vikus and Solovet returned just as the food was ready. They looked worried.

Everyone gathered around as Mareth passed out fish, bread, and something that reminded Gregor of a sweet potato but wasn't.

"Boots! Dinnertime!" said Gregor, and she ran over.

When she realized they weren't following, she turned her head and waved impatiently to the roaches. "Temp! Ticka! Din-uh!"

An awkward social moment. No one else had thought to invite the roaches. Mareth had not prepared enough food. Clearly it wasn't standard to dine with roaches. Fortunately they shook their heads. "No, Princess, we eat not now." They started to scurry away.

"Stay dere!" said Boots, pointing at Temp and Tick. "You stay dere, beeg bugs." And the roaches obediently sat down.

"Boots!" said Gregor, embarrassed. "You don't have to stay — she orders everybody around," he told the roaches. "It's just she wants to keep playing with you but she has to eat first."

"We will sit," said one stiffly, and Gregor had the feeling the bug wanted him to mind his own business.

Everyone ate hungrily except Vikus, who seemed distracted.

"So when leave we?" asked Henry, through a mouthful of fish.

"We do not," said Solovet. "The crawlers have refused to come."

Luxa's head snapped up indignantly. "Refused? On what grounds?"

"They do not wish to invite the anger of King Gorger by joining our quest," said Vikus. "They have peace with both humans and rats now. They do not want to unseat it."

"Now what?" thought Gregor. They needed two roaches. It said so in "The Prophecy of Gray." If the roaches didn't come, could they still rescue his father?

"We have asked them to rethink the proposition," said Solovet. "They know the rats are on the march. This may sway them in our direction."

"Or in the rats'," muttered Luxa, and Gregor secretly agreed. The roaches had debated trading Overlanders to the rats even when they knew the rats would eat them. And that was yesterday when there was no war. If Boots hadn't been so appealing, no doubt they would be dead now. The roaches weren't fighters. Gregor thought they would do what was best for their species, and the rats were probably the stronger ally. Or they would be if you could trust them.

"What makes the roaches think they can believe the rats?" asked Gregor.

"The crawlers do not think in the same manner we do," said Vikus.

"How do they think?" asked Gregor.

"Without reason or consequence," Henry broke in angrily. "They are the stupidest of creatures in the Underland! Why, they can barely even speak!"

"Silence, Henry!" said Vikus sharply.

Gregor glanced back at Temp and Tick, but the roaches gave no sign they had heard. Of course they had. The roaches didn't seem too bright, but it was just rude to say it in front of them. Besides, that wasn't going to make them want to come along.

"Remember you, when Sandwich arrived in the Underland the crawlers had been here for countless generations. No doubt they will remain when all thought of warm blood has passed," said Vikus.

"That is rumor," said Henry dismissively.

"No, it's not. Cockroaches have been around, like, three hundred and fifty million years, and people haven't even been here six," said Gregor. His dad had showed him a time line of when different animals had evolved on Earth. He remembered being impressed by how old cockroaches were.

"How do you know this?" Luxa spoke abruptly, but Gregor could tell she was actually interested.

"It's science. Archaeologists dig up fossils and stuff, and they can tell how old things are. Cockroaches — I mean crawlers — are really old and they've never changed much," said Gregor. He was getting on shaky ground here, but he thought that was true. "They're pretty amazing." He hoped Temp and Tick were listening.

Vikus smiled at him. "For a creature to survive so long, it is, no doubt, as smart as it need be."

"I do not believe in your science," said Henry. "The crawlers are weak, they cannot fight, they will not last. That is how nature intended it."

Gregor thought of his grandma, who was old and dependent on the kindness of stronger people now. He thought of Boots, who was little and couldn't yet open a door. And there was his friend Larry, who had to go to the hospital emergency room three times last year when his asthma flared up and he couldn't get air into his lungs.

"Is that what you think, Luxa?" said Gregor. "Do you think something deserves to die if it's not strong?"

"It does not matter what I think, if that is the truth," said Luxa evasively.

"But is it the truth? That is an excellent question for the future ruler of Regalia to ponder," said Vikus.

They ate quickly and Vikus suggested they all try to sleep. Gregor had no idea if it was night or not but he felt tired and didn't object.

While he spread out a thin, woven blanket at the edge of the chamber, Boots tried to teach Temp and Tick to play Patty-Cake. The roaches waved their front legs in confusion, not understanding what was going on.

"Pat cake, pat cake, baka man. Bake me cake fast you can. Pat it, pick it, mark wif a B. Put in ofen for Beeg Bug and me!" sang Boots as she clapped and touched the roaches' feet.

The bugs were completely baffled. "What sings the princess, what sings?" asked Temp. Or maybe it was Tick.

"It's a song we sing with babies in the Overland," said Gregor. "She put you in it. That's a big honor," he said. "She only puts someone in a song if she really likes them."

"Me like Beeg Bug," said Boots with satisfaction, and sang the song again with the roaches.

"Sorry, guys, she has to sleep now," said Gregor. "Come on, Boots. Sleepy time. Say good night."

Boots spontaneously hugged the roaches. "Night, Beeg Bug. Seep tight." Gregor was glad she left out "don't let the bedbugs bite."

Gregor snuggled down with her under the blanket on the hard stone floor. After her long nap, she wasn't very sleepy. He let her play with the flashlight awhile, clicking it on and off, but he was afraid she'd run down the batteries, and it was making the Underlanders restless. Finally he got her to settle down and sleep. As he drifted off, he thought he heard Temp, or maybe it was Tick, whispering, "Honors us, the princess, honors us?"

He didn't know what woke him. By the stiffness in his neck, he must've been lying on the hard floor for hours. He drowsily reached over to pull Boots's warm body next to him but he found only cold stone. His eyes snapped open and he sat up. His lips parted to call her name as his vision came into focus. No sound came out.

Boots was in the center of the big round chamber, rocking from foot to foot as she turned calmly in a circle. The flashlight she held illuminated the room in sections. He could see the figures stretching out in every direction in perfect concentric rings. They swayed in unison, some to the left, some to the right, with slow, mesmerizing movements.

In total silence, hundreds of cockroaches were dancing around Boots.

CHAPTER

15

"Oh, geez, they're going to eat her!" thought Gregor, springing to his feet and smacking his head into the ceiling. "Ow!" It had been a mistake to take off his hard hat to sleep.

A hand grasped his shoulder to steady him, and he made out Vikus with a finger pressed to his lips. "Sh! Halt them not!" he whispered urgently.

"But they're going to hurt her!" Gregor whispered back. He hunched down and put a hand to his head. He could feel a big lump already rising out of his scalp.

"No, Gregor, they honor her. They honor Boots in a manner most sacred and rare," whispered Solovet from somewhere next to Vikus.

Gregor looked back at the roaches and tried to make sense of it. Boots didn't seem in any immediate danger.

None of the bugs was actually touching her. They just swayed and turned and bowed in their slow, rhythmic dance. There was something else, the solemnity of the scene, the complete silence, the absorption. It hit him: The roaches weren't just honoring Boots — they were *worshiping* her!

"What are they doing?" Gregor asked.

"It is the Ring Dance. It is said the crawlers perform it only in the greatest secrecy for ones they believe to be chosen," answered Vikus. "In our history, they have only performed it for one other human, and that was Sandwich."

"Chosen for what?" whispered Gregor, worried. He hoped the cockroaches didn't think they could keep Boots just because they did some dance around her.

"Chosen to give them time," said Vikus simply, as if that explained it all. Gregor translated that in his head to mean "chosen to give them life."

Maybe it was something simpler. From the moment they'd landed in the Underland, the roaches had felt a special connection to Boots. If they'd just found him, he'd have had a one-way ticket to the rats, end of story. But Boots had befriended them so quickly. She hadn't been repulsed or superior or scared. Gregor thought the fact that she had liked the roaches had made a great impression on them. Most of the humans had such a low opinion of them.

Then there was that strange thing about recognizing Temp. . . . He still couldn't explain that.

The roaches did a series of turns and landed flat on the ground facing Boots. Then, circle by circle, they melted away into the darkness. Boots watched them go without comment. When the chamber had cleared, she gave a head-splitting yawn and padded over to Gregor. "I seepy," she said. Then she curled up against him and nodded right off.

Gregor took the flashlight from her hand and in its beam saw that all the other Underlanders were awake, staring at them. "She's sleepy," he said as if nothing unusual had happened. He clicked off the light.

When they woke, the roaches announced that Temp and Tick would be joining the quest. There was no doubt in anyone's mind that they were coming because of Boots.

Gregor was torn between being very proud and wanting to laugh his head off. It turned out Boots was special weaponry after all.

The party quickly readied itself to depart. Temp and Tick absolutely refused to ride on any bat without Boots. This caused a brief argument because Boots had to ride with Gregor and that meant one bat had to carry both the Overlanders and the roaches. The bats could handle the load, but it meant four inexperienced fliers would be alone on one bat.

Vikus gave the job to Henry's big black bat, Ares, as he was both strong and agile, and Henry rode with Luxa. Ares was instructed to fly above the others just in case one of the roaches fell off and had to be caught before it hit the ground.

None of this talk seemed to relax Temp and Tick, who were obviously terrified at the idea of soaring through wide-open spaces high above the ground. Gregor found himself trying to reassure them, which was ironic since he didn't much like flying, either. He also wished he could have any bat but Ares. Henry's bat probably disliked him as much as Henry did.

They didn't have time for breakfast, but Mareth passed out chunks of cake and dried beef to eat on the journey. Vikus told Gregor they would be flying several hours before they took a break, so he put a second diaper over Boots's first one. He also repositioned her in the backpack so that she was looking backward instead of over his shoulder — that way, she could chatter with Temp and Tick and maybe distract them from their fear.

Gregor gingerly climbed up on Ares's back and dangled his legs off the bat's shoulders. Temp and Tick scrambled on behind and clung to Ares's back fur for dear life. Gregor thought he saw the bat wince a little, but Ares didn't say anything. The bats hardly ever spoke out loud, though. It seemed to require a lot of effort. They probably talked to one another in squeaks too high for human ears to hear.

"We must now travel to the land of the spinners," said Vikus. "Remember how frequently the rats patrol this area."

"Fly close together. We may have need of one another's protection," said Solovet. "To the air!"

The bats took off. Boots was pleased as punch with her new traveling companions. She sang her whole repertoire of songs, which included "Twinkle, Twinkle Little Star"; "Hey, Diddle, Diddle"; "The Itsy-Bitsy Spider"; "The Alphabet Song"; and, of course "Patty-Cake, Patty-Cake." Having finished, she sang them again. And again. And again. On about the nineteenth round, Gregor decided to teach her "Row, Row, Row Your Boat" just for a little variety. Boots picked it up immediately and then tried to teach it to the roaches. She didn't seem to mind their off-key voices, although Gregor could feel the muscles in Ares's neck getting tighter with each verse.

Gregor could tell the roaches' domain sprawled over a much larger area than Regalia or the bats' caves. The humans and bats had small, densely populated lands that could be protected easily. The roaches lived across miles and miles of the Underland.

How did they keep themselves safe from attack with all this space to defend?

The answer came to him as they flew over a valley that held thousands of roaches. The crawlers had numbers — huge numbers, compared with the humans. If they were attacked, they could afford to lose more fighters. And with so much space, they could retreat endlessly and make the rats follow them. Gregor thought about the roaches in their kitchen at home. They didn't fight. They ran for it. His mom swatted a lot of them, but they always came back.

After what seemed like an eternity, Gregor felt Ares coasting in for a landing. They settled down on the bank of a lazy, shallow river. Gregor hopped off and onto something soft and spongy. He reached down to investigate, and his hand came up filled with a grayish- green, leafy vine. Plants! Plants grew down here without the help of the gaslight the Underlanders used.

"How does this grow without the light?" he asked Vikus, holding out a handful of the stuff.

"It has light," said Vikus, pointing into the river. "There is fire from the earth." Gregor peered into the water and saw tiny jets of light shooting out of the river bottom. Fish darted in and out of a variety of plant-life. The long vines of certain plants crept onto the banks.

"Oh, they're like miniature volcanoes," thought Gregor.

"This river runs through Regalia as well. Our cattle live off the plants, but they are unfit for humans to eat," said Solovet.

Gregor had been eating beef jerky all morning without wondering what the cows ate. He could probably spend years in the Underland figuring out how it worked. Not that he wanted to.

Cockroaches who were fishing along the banks had a quick exchange with Temp and Tick and pulled several large fish out of the river with their mouths. Mareth cleaned them and set them on the torches to grill.

Gregor set Boots down to stretch her legs and asked the cockroaches to keep an eye on her. They ran up and down the bank steering her away from the water and letting her ride on their backs. Word of her arrival spread quickly, and soon dozens of bugs appeared. They settled down just to watch "the princess."

When the food was cooked, Vikus made a point of inviting Temp and Tick to join them. "It is time," he said in response to Henry's frown. "It is time those of the prophecy became of one journey, of one purpose, of one mind. All are equal here." Temp and Tick still sat off to the side, behind Boots, but they ate with everyone else.

"It is not far now," said Vikus, pointing at a small tunnel. "One could make it shortly even on foot."

"To my dad?" asked Gregor.

"No, to the spinners. We must persuade two to join us on the quest," said Vikus.

"Oh, yeah. The spinners," said Gregor. He hoped they were more into the trip than the roaches had been.

They were just finishing up the meal when all five bats jerked their heads up. "Rats!" hissed Ares, and everyone started moving.

Except for Temp and Tick, all the roaches vanished into the shallow tunnels that led away from the riverbank.

Vikus thrust Boots into Gregor's backpack and shoved them toward the tunnel he had pointed out earlier. "Run!" he ordered. Gregor tried to object, but Vikus cut him off. "Run, Gregor! The rest of us are expendable; you are not!"

The old man vaulted onto his bat and joined the other Underlanders in the air just as a squad of six rats stampeded onto the riverbank. The leader, a gnarled gray rat with a diagonal scar across his face, pointed at Gregor and hissed, "Kill him!"

Stranded on the riverbank without a weapon, Gregor had no choice but to sprint for the mouth of the tunnel. Temp and Tick scurried after him. He glanced back for a second and saw Vikus knock the scarred rat into the river with the hilt of his sword. The other Underlanders, blades flashing, were attacking the five remaining rats.

"Run, Gregor!" ordered Solovet in a rough voice so unlike the quiet one he was used to.

"Make haste, make you, make haste!" urged Temp and Tick.

Using his flashlight, Gregor started down the tunnel. It was just high enough that he could run upright. He realized he had lost Temp and Tick somewhere and turned back to see the entire tunnel, floor to ceiling, filling up with roaches. They weren't attacking the rats. They were using their bodies to form a barricade that would be nearly impossible to penetrate.

"Oh, no," thought Gregor. "They're just going to let themselves be killed!" He turned back to help them, but the roaches nearest him insisted, "Run! Run with the princess!"

They were right: He had to go. He had to get Boots out of there. He had to save his dad. Maybe he even had to save the Underland from the rats, he didn't know. But right now he could no more get through the fifty-foot wall of cockroaches to fight the rats than the rats could get to him.

He took off down the tunnel, setting a pace he thought he could maintain for half an hour.

At twenty minutes he turned a corner and ran straight into an enormous spiderweb.

CHAPTER

16

He ripped his face off the sticky ropes, and it felt like someone had yanked strips of adhesive tape off his skin. "Ow!" he said. He freed his flashlight arm, but the other remained enmeshed in the web. Boots was on his back, so she hadn't got caught.

"Hello!" he called. "Is anyone there? Hello!" He shone the flashlight around, but all he could see was web.

"I am Gregor the Overlander. I come in peace," he said. I come in peace. Where'd he get that? Probably from some old movie. "Anybody home?"

He felt a light tugging on his sandals and looked down. A huge spider was wrapping his feet together with a steady stream of silk.

"Hey!" yelled Gregor, trying to free his feet. But in seconds the spider had spun its way up to his knees. "You don't understand! I'm — I'm the warrior! In the prophecy! I'm the one who calls!"

The spider busily worked its way up his body. "Oh, man," thought Gregor. "It's going to cover us completely!" He felt the arm that was caught in the web tighten up against his body.

"Ge-go!" squeaked Boots. The silk ropes pressed her against his back as they encircled his chest.

"Vikus sent me!" yelled Gregor, and for the first time the spider paused. He quickly followed up. "Yeah, Vikus sent me and he's on his way and he's going to be really mad you're wrapping us up!"

He waved his free arm with the flashlight for emphasis and caught the spider full in the face with the light. It skittered back a few yards, and Gregor got his first good look at the arachnid. Six beady black eyes, bristly legs, and massive jaws that ended in curved, pointed fangs. He quickly diverted the flashlight beam. No point in making it angry.

"So, do you know Vikus?" he asked. "He should be here any minute to have some official meeting with your king. Queen. Do you guys have a king or a queen? Or maybe it's something else. We have a president, but that's different because you have to vote for them." He paused. "So, do you think you could unwrap us now?"

The spider leaned down and snapped a thread with its jaws. Gregor and Boots shot up fifty feet in the air and yo-yoed up and down like they were on a big rubber band. "Hey!" Gregor yelled. "Hey!" His lunch sloshed around in his stomach. Eventually the bouncing stopped.

Gregor shone the flashlight around him. In every direction he could see spiders. Some were working busily; others seemed asleep. Every single one of them was ignoring him. This was new. The roaches and bats had greeted him civilly enough, a whole crowd of people in the stadium had fallen silent when he appeared, and the rats had gone into a rage when they'd met . . . but the spiders? They couldn't care less.

He yelled stuff at them for a while. Nice stuff. Crazy stuff. Annoying stuff. They didn't react. He got Boots to sing a couple rounds of "The Itsy-Bitsy Spider" since she had a special way with bugs. No response. Finally he just gave up and watched them.

An unlucky insect flew into their web. A spider ran over and drove its wicked fangs into the bug. It went still. "Poison," thought Gregor. The spider quickly wrapped the insect in silk, broke it into pieces, and shot some kind of juice inside it. Gregor looked away when the spider started sucking out the bug's liquefied insides. "Ugh, that could've been us. That still could be us!" he thought. He wished Vikus and the others would show up.

But would they show up? What had happened back on the riverbank? Had they been able to fight off the rats? Had anybody been hurt, or worse, killed?

He remembered Vikus's ordering him to run. "The rest of us are expendable, you are not!" He must have been talking about the prophecy. They could always find more crawlers, fliers, and spinners. Nerissa might be able to stand in if something happened to Luxa or Henry. Or maybe they would make someone else the king or queen. But Gregor and Boots, two Overlanders with a dad imprisoned by rats, they were irreplaceable.

Gregor thought grimly of the people sacrificing themselves back on the riverbank. He should have stayed and fought even if he didn't stand much of a chance. They were risking their lives because they thought he was the warrior. But he wasn't. Surely that was clear by now.

Minutes dragged by. Maybe the whole party had been wiped out and he and Boots were on their own. Maybe the spiders knew that and they were just letting them live so they could be nice and fresh when they decided to eat them.

"Ge-go?" said Boots.

"Yeah, Boots," said Gregor.

"We go home?" she asked plaintively. "See Mama?"

"Well, we have to get Daddy first," he said, trying to sound optimistic even though they were dangling helplessly in a spider's lair.

"Da-da?" said Boots curiously. She knew their father from photos, though she'd never seen him in person. "See Da-da?"

"We get Da-da. Then we go home," said Gregor.

"See Mama?" Boots insisted. Images of their mom began to make Gregor ache with sadness. "See Mama?"

A spider near them began to make a humming sound that was picked up by the other creatures. It was a soothing, soft melody. Gregor tried to remember the tune so he could play it for his dad on his saxophone. His dad played, too. Jazz, mostly. He'd bought Gregor his first saxophone, a used one from the pawnshop, when he was seven and started teaching him to play it. Gregor had just begun lessons at school when his dad had dropped out of sight and become a prisoner of the rats who probably hated music.

What were the rats doing to his dad, anyway?

He tried to distract himself with more positive thoughts but, given the circumstances, failed.

When Henry materialized on the stone floor below him, Gregor wanted to cry with relief. "He lives!" Henry called out, looking genuinely happy to see him.

From somewhere in the darkness Gregor heard Vikus call out, "Free you the Overlander, free you?" He felt himself being lowered to the ground. When his feet hit the stone, he fell on his stomach, unable to stand on his wrapped legs.

They instantly gathered around him, cutting the silk off with their swords. Even Luxa and Henry helped. Tick and Temp chewed through the cords around Boots's pack. Gregor counted the bats, one, two, three, four, five. He could see several wounds, but everybody was alive.

"We thought you lost," said Mareth, who was bleeding freely from his thigh.

"No, I couldn't get lost. The tunnel came straight here," said Gregor, kicking his legs free happily.

"Not lost in direction," said Luxa. "Lost forever." Gregor realized she meant dead.

"What happened with the rats?" he asked.

"All killed," said Vikus. "You need not fear that they have seen you."

"It's worse if they see me?" asked Gregor. "Why? They

140

can smell I'm an Overlander from miles away. They know I'm here."

"But only the dead ones know you resemble your father. That you are 'a son of the sun,'" said Vikus. Gregor remembered how Fangor and Shed had reacted when they'd seen his face in the torchlight. "Mark you, Shed, his shade?" They hadn't just wanted to kill him because he was an Overlander. They'd thought he was the warrior, too! He wanted to tell Vikus about that, but a score of spiders were descending around them and perching in nearby webs.

One magnificent creature with beautifully striped legs swung down directly in front of Vikus. He bowed very low. "Greetings, Queen Wevox."

The spider rubbed her front legs over her chest as if she were playing the harp. An eerie voice came out of her although there was no movement of her mouth. "Greetings, Lord Vikus."

"Meet you, Gregor the Overlander, meet you," said Vikus, indicating Gregor.

"He makes much noise," said the queen distastefully, her front legs moving across her chest again. Gregor realized that was how she talked, by making vibrations on her body. She sounded sort of like Mr. Johnson in apartment 4Q who'd had some kind of operation and talked through a hole in his neck. Only scary.

"The Overlander ways are odd," said Vikus, shooting Gregor a look that told him not to object.

"Why come you?" strummed Queen Wevox.

Vikus told the whole tale in ten sentences using a soft

voice. So apparently you spoke to spiders quickly and quietly. Screaming at them endlessly had been counterproductive.

The queen considered the story a moment. "As it is Vikus, we will not drink. Web them."

A horde of spiders surrounded them. Gregor watched a gorgeous, gauzy funnel of silk grow up around them as if by magic. It isolated the party and blocked all else from view. The spiders stopped spinning when it reached thirty feet. Two took positions as sentries at the top. It all happened in under a minute.

Everyone looked at Vikus, who sighed. "You knew it would not be simple," said Solovet gently.

"Yes, but I had hoped with the recent trade agreement . . ." Vikus trailed off. "I hoped too high."

"We still breathe," said Mareth encouragingly. "That is no small thing with the spinners."

"What's going on?" said Gregor. "Aren't they coming with us?"

"No, Gregor," said Solovet. "We are their prisoners."

CHAPTER

17

"Prisoners!" exclaimed Gregor. "Are you at war with the spiders, too?"

"Oh, no," said Mareth. "We are on peaceful terms with the spinners. We trade with them, we do not invade each other's lands . . . but it would be an exaggeration to call them our friends."

"I'll say," said Gregor. "So, did everybody know they would lock us up except me?" He had trouble keeping the irritation out of his voice. He was getting tired of finding out about things after the fact.

"I am sorry, Gregor," said Vikus. "I have worked long to build bridges between ourselves and the spinners. I thought perhaps they would be more agreeable, but I overestimated my influence with them."

He looked weary and old. Gregor hadn't meant to make

him feel worse than he already did. "No, they really respect you. I mean, I think they were going to eat me until I mentioned your name."

Vikus brightened a little. "Truly? Well, that is something. Where there is life there is hope."

"That's so weird. That's what my grandma always says!" said Gregor. He laughed, and somehow that broke the tension.

"Ge-go, fesh di-pur!" said Boots crankily. She tugged at her pants.

"Yes, Boots, fresh diaper," said Gregor. She hadn't been changed for ages. He dug through the pack Dulcet had given him and realized he was down to two diapers. "Uh-oh," he said. "I'm almost out of catch cloths."

"Well, you could not be in a better place. The spinners weave all our catch cloths," said Solovet.

"How come they're not sticky?" asked Gregor, touching his face.

"Spinners can make six different kinds of silk, some sticky, some soft as Boots's skin. They make our garments as well."

"Really?" said Gregor. "Do you think they'd let us have more catch cloths? Even if we're prisoners?"

"I doubt it not. It is not the spiders' goal to antagonize us," said Solovet. "Only to hold us until they can determine what to do." She called up to a guard, and in a few minutes two dozen diapers came down on a thread. The spider also sent down three woven baskets filled with clean water.

Solovet began to work her way around the group, cleaning

wounds and patching people up. Luxa, Henry, and Mareth paid close attention, as if she were teaching a class. Gregor realized the ability to heal battle wounds was probably important if you lived down here.

Solovet began by cleaning the gash on Mareth's thigh and stitching it up with a needle and thread. Gregor winced on Mareth's behalf, but the guard's face was pale and set. Two bats required stitches on torn wings and, though they made a great effort to remain still while Solovet slid the needle in and out of their skin, the process was clearly agonizing for them.

Once all obvious bleeding had been stopped, Solovet turned to Gregor. "Let us attend to your face now."

Gregor touched his cheek and found that welts had formed where the webs had ripped off. Solovet soaked a catch cloth in water and placed it on his face. Gregor had to grit his teeth to keep from screaming.

"I know it burns," said Solovet. "But you must wash the glue from your skin or it will fester."

"Fester?" said Gregor. That sounded awful.

"If you could stand to splash water upon your face, it would be a more painful but faster process," said Solovet.

Gregor took a deep breath and dunked his whole head into one of the baskets of water. "Aaaa!" he screamed silently, and came up gasping. After five or six dunks, the pain faded.

Solovet nodded approvingly and gave him a small clay pot of ointment to dab on his face. While he gingerly applied the medicine, she cleaned and bound a series of smaller wounds and forced an uncooperative Vikus to let her wrap his wrist.

Finally she turned to Temp and Tick. "Crawlers, need you any assistance from me?"

Boots pointed out a bent antenna on one of the roaches. "Temp boo-boo," she said.

"No, Princess, we heal ourselves," said Temp. Gregor was sorry Temp was injured but, on the plus side, he could now tell the roaches apart.

"Ban-didge!" insisted Boots, and reached out to grab the crooked antenna.

"No, Boots!" said Gregor, blocking her hand. "No bandage on Temp."

"Ban-didge!" Boots gave Gregor a scowl and pushed him away.

"Oh, great," thought Gregor. "Here we go." In general, Boots was a very good-natured two-year-old. But she was still two and, every so often, she would throw a tantrum that left the rest of the family exhausted. Usually it happened when she was tired and hungry.

Gregor dug in the pack. Hadn't Dulcet said something about treats? He pulled out a cookie. "Cookie, Boots?" She reluctantly took the cookie and sat down to gnaw on it. Maybe he had headed off the worst.

"Hates us, the princess, hates us?" asked Tick worriedly.

"Oh, no," said Gregor. "She just gets like this sometimes. My mom calls it the terrible twos. Sometimes she throws a fit for no reason."

Boots scowled at everybody and drummed her feet on

the ground.

"Hates us, the princess, hates us?" murmured Temp sadly.

Baby roaches probably didn't have tantrums.

"No, really, she still thinks you're great," promised Gregor. "Just give her some space." He hoped the roaches wouldn't get so hurt by Boots's behavior that they'd want to go home. Not that anyone was going anywhere right now.

Vikus gestured him over to where the others had gathered. He spoke in a whisper. "Gregor, my wife fears the spinners may pass on our whereabouts to the rats. She advises that we escape with all speed."

"I'm good with that!" said Gregor. "But how?" Boots came up behind him and gave his arm a pinch for no reason. "No, Boots!" he said. "No pinching!"

"More cookie!" she said, tugging on him.

"No, not for pinchers. Cookies are not for pinchers," said Gregor firmly. Her lower lip began to tremble. She marched away from him, plunked herself down on the floor, and began to kick at the pack.

"Okay, sorry, what? What's the plan?" said Gregor, turning back to the group. "Can we just cut our way through the web and run?"

"No, outside this funnel web are scores of spinners ready to repair a hole and attack with poison fang. If we flee upward, they will leap on us from above," whispered Solovet.

"What's that leave?" said Gregor.

"Only one resort. We must damage the web so fully and

147

so rapidly, they cannot repair it nor will it hold their weight," said Solovet. She paused. "Someone must perform the Coiler."

Everyone looked at Luxa, so Gregor looked at her, too. Her golden bat, which stood behind her, dipped its head down and touched her neck. "We can do it," said Luxa softly.

"We do not insist, Luxa. The danger, particularly at the top, is very great. But in truth, you are our best hope," said Vikus unhappily.

Henry put his arm around her shoulder. "They can do it. I have seen them in training. They have both speed and accuracy."

Luxa nodded resolutely. "We can do it. Let us not wait."

"Gregor, ride you on Vikus's bat. Vikus, with me. Henry and Mareth, take one crawler each," said Solovet.

"We need a distraction to cover Luxa," said Mareth. "I could go through the side."

"Not with that leg," said Solovet, her eyes flashing around. "And no one goes through the side. It is certain death."

"The spinners are very sensitive to noise," said Vikus. "It is too bad we have no horns."

Gregor felt a pair of feet drumming angrily into his legs. He turned around and saw Boots on the floor kicking him. "Cut it out!" he snapped at her. "Do you need a time-out?"

"No time-out! You time-out! You time-out! Cookie! Cookie!" sputtered Boots. She was about to blow any minute.

"You need a noise?" said Gregor in frustration. "I've got a noise for you." He picked Boots up and wrestled her into the backpack.

"No! No! No!" Boots said, her voice rising in pitch and intensity.

"Everybody ready?" asked Gregor, pulling a cookie from Dulcet's bag.

The Underlanders weren't exactly sure what he was doing, but in seconds they were prepared to take off.

Solovet gave him a nod. "We are ready."

Gregor held up the cookie. "Hey, Boots!" said Gregor. "Want a cookie?"

"No, cookie, no, cookie, no, no, no!" said Boots, way past the point of being pacified.

"Okay," said Gregor. "Then I'll eat it." And making sure she could see, he stuck the whole cookie in his mouth.

"Mine!" screamed Boots. "Mine! Mine! Miiiiiiiiine!" It was an eardrum-piercing shriek that rattled his brain.

"Go you, Luxa!" cried Solovet, and the girl took off on her bat. Now Gregor could understand why the Coiler was such a big deal. Luxa was rising up along the web spinning and twisting at a dizzying rate. She held her sword out straight above her head. It was slicing the funnel to shreds. Only an extraordinary and flexible rider could have pulled off a move like that.

"Wow!" said Gregor. He jumped on Vikus's big gray bat.

"Miiiiiiine!" screeched Boots. "Miiiiine!"

Above him he could see Luxa spinning and slicing. The other Underlanders were following her, cutting straight up the sides of the funnel web. Gregor brought up the rear with Boots and her blinding screams.

At the top of the funnel, the golden bat hung in space performing an intricate, upside-down figure eight. Under the protection of Luxa's flashing sword, the Underlanders zipped out to freedom.

Gregor was the only one still in the funnel when it happened. From above, a jet of silk shot down, encircling Luxa's sword arm and jerking her from her bat. The pair of striped legs reeled her in like a fish.

The fangs of Queen Wevox opened to receive Luxa's neck.

CHAPTER 18

Gregor's mouth dropped open in horror. Luxa was seconds away from dying. She knew it, too. She was writhing in terror, trying to bite through the silk rope at her wrist with her teeth, but it was too strong.

He felt around desperately for a weapon. What did he have? Diapers? Cookies? Oh, why hadn't they given him a sword? He was the stupid warrior, wasn't he? His fingers dug in the leather bag and closed around the root beer can. Root beer! He yanked out the can shaking it with all his might. "Attack! Attack!" he yelled.

Just as the fangs were about to pierce Luxa's throat, he flew up and popped the soda can top. The stream of root beer shot out and smacked the spider queen right in the face. She dropped Luxa and began to claw at her six eyes.

Luxa fell and was swept up by her bat. They joined the

rest of the Underlanders who were fighting their way back to help.

"Blade Wheel!" commanded Solovet, and the bats formed into the tight flying circle that had surrounded Gregor when he'd tried to escape from the stadium. The humans extended their swords straight out to the sides, and the formation began to move through the air like a buzz saw.

Boots's unearthly shrieks were causing many of the spiders to curl up in cowering balls. Whether it was the noise, the Blade Wheel, or fear of the root beer, Gregor didn't know. All he knew was that in a few minutes they were flying free and leaving the spiders far behind.

Gregor unclenched his legs when he realized he was probably squeezing the life out of his bat. In one hand he still held the half-empty can of root beer. He would have taken a drink if he'd thought he could swallow.

Boots's screams soon became whimpers. She put her head on his shoulder and crashed. She'd been so upset, she still made little gasping sounds in her sleep. Gregor turned and placed a kiss on her curly head.

Luxa was stretched out on her bat's back alive but wiped out. He saw Solovet and Vikus flying near her, speaking. She nodded but didn't sit up. They took the lead, and the bats sped even faster into the darkness.

They flew a long time down deserted passages. Gregor saw no sign of life, either animal or plant. Eventually, Solovet and Vikus waved them down, and the party landed in a vast cavern at the mouth of a tunnel.

Everybody practically fell off the bats and just lay on the

ground. Temp and Tick seemed almost comatose from fear. The bats staggered together and pressed into a tight, trembling knot.

After a while, Gregor heard himself speak up. "So, isn't it time I had a sword?"

There was a moment of silence, then all the Underlanders burst out laughing. They went on and on. Gregor didn't really get the joke, but he laughed along with them, feeling the darkness drain out of his body.

The laughter woke Boots, who rubbed her eyes and said cheerfully, "Where spider?"

Somehow that set everybody off again. Pleased with the response, Boots kept repeating, "Where spider? Where spider?" to appreciative laughter.

"Spider go bye-bye," said Gregor finally. "How about a cookie?"

"Ye-es!" said Boots, without a trace of anger over the earlier cookie incident. That was one great thing about her. Once she'd melted down and napped, she transformed back into her own sweet self again.

When they realized the princess did not in fact hate them, Temp and Tick rallied and ran around playing tag with her.

Mareth started to prepare food, but Solovet ordered him to lie down and prop up his leg. She and Vikus made dinner while Henry and Mareth played some kind of card game.

Gregor went over to Luxa, who was sitting on a stone ledge. He sat beside her and could feel she was still shaking. "How are you doing?" he asked.

"I am fine," she said in a tight voice.

"That was really cool, that Coiler thing you did," he said.

"It was my first time in a real web," confessed Luxa.

"Mine, too. Of course, in the Overland, spinners are small, and we don't call them our neighbors," said Gregor.

Luxa grimaced. "We do not mix much with spinners."

"Well, that's probably a good thing. I mean, who wants to mix with somebody who spends the whole time thinking about drinking you?" Gregor said.

Luxa looked shocked. "You would not joke so had the queen trapped you!"

"Hey, I was hanging there yelling for an hour before you guys decided to show up," said Gregor. "And they really hated me."

Luxa laughed. "I could tell. By what Queen Wevox said." She paused. Her next words were an effort. "Thank you."

"For what?" he said.

"Saving me with the . . . What is this weapon?" She gestured to the root beer can.

"It's not a weapon. It's a root beer," Gregor said. He took a swig.

Luxa looked alarmed. "Should you drink it?" she asked.

"Sure, try it," he said. Gregor offered her the can.

She tentatively took a sip, and her eyes widened. "It bubbles on the tongue," she said.

"Yeah, that's why it exploded. I shook up a lot of bubbles. It's safe now. It's just like water. Go ahead, you can finish it," he said, and she continued to take tiny curious sips.

"Anyway, I owed you one," he said. "You saved me from that rat the first night. So we're even."

Luxa nodded but seemed troubled. "There is one other thing. I should not have struck you for trying to escape. I am sorry."

"And I'm sorry I called your home creepy. It's not like it's all creepy. Some of it's great," he said.

"Am I 'creepy' to you?" asked Luxa.

"Oh, no. Creepy is like spiders and rats and, you know, things that make chills run down your spine. You're just . . . difficult," said Gregor, trying to be honest but not flat-out rude.

"You, too. You are difficult to . . . uh . . . make do things," said Luxa.

Gregor nodded, but he rolled his eyes when she wasn't looking. It was hard to imagine anyone more stubborn than Luxa.

Vikus called them all to dine, and even the roaches felt comfortable enough to join the circle.

"I am drinking Gregor's spinner weapon," announced Luxa, holding up the root beer can. He had to explain about the root beer all over again, and then everybody had to try a sip.

When the can got to Boots, he said, "Well, that's the end of that," thinking she'd guzzled down the last few swallows. But instead she poured out two little puddles.

"Beeg bugs," she said, pointing to the first puddle. "Bats," she said, pointing to the second. Both sets of animals obligingly drank up the root beer.

"I believe Boots to be a natural ambassador," said Vikus, smiling. "She treats all with an equality I myself aspire to. Come, let us eat."

Everyone dug in like they'd never seen food before. When he'd slowed down enough to actually taste his food, Gregor asked the question that had been worrying him since they'd escaped from the spiders. "Can we still go on the quest without the spinners?"

"That is the question," said Vikus. "That is the question we must all consider. Clearly we cannot expect any spinners to join us willingly."

"We should have seized two when we had a chance," said Henry darkly.

"The prophecy says the spinners must assent," said Vikus. "However, we know the rats have taken many spinners prisoner. Perhaps we can free a few and persuade them to accompany us. I have often had good results with spinners."

"But you will not be there, Vikus," Solovet said quietly.

"What do you mean?" asked Gregor, feeling his mouth go dry.

Vikus paused a moment, taking in the group. "It is time for those of us not named by the prophecy to return home. Mareth, Solovet, and I will fly after we rest."

Gregor saw his surprise mirrored on Luxa's and Henry's faces.

"Nothing in the prophecy forbids you to come," said Luxa.

"We are not meant to be here. And beyond that we have a war to fight," said Solovet.

The thought of going anywhere without Vikus and Solovet filled Gregor with panic. "But you can't leave us. I mean, we don't even know where we're going," said Gregor. "Do you guys know where we're going?" he asked Luxa and Henry. They both shook their heads. "See?"

"You will manage. Henry and Luxa are well trained, and you show great resourcefulness," said Solovet. She spoke simply and definitely. She was thinking of the war, of the bigger picture, not of them.

Gregor instinctively knew he could not change her mind. He turned to Vikus. "You can't leave. We need you. We need someone — someone who knows what they're doing!"

He looked at Luxa and Henry to see if they were insulted, but both were waiting anxiously for Vikus's reply. "They know," thought Gregor. "They act tough, but they know we can't get through this by ourselves."

"I do not plan to leave you stranded in the Dead Land," said Vikus.

"Oh, great, and we're in the Dead Land," said Gregor. "So, you're going to . . . what? Draw us a map?"

"No, I have arranged a guide for you," said Vikus.

"A guide?" asked Henry.

"A guide?" echoed Luxa.

Vikus took a deep breath as if he was about to begin a long explanation. But then someone interrupted him.

"Well, I prefer to think of myself as a legend, but I suppose 'guide' will do," said a deep, world-weary voice from the dark.

Gregor shot his flashlight beam toward the sound.

157

Leaning in the mouth of the tunnel was a rat with a diagonal scar across his face. It took just a moment for Gregor to recognize him as the rat Vikus had knocked into the river.

PART 3

THE RAT

CHAPTER

19

"Stay you!" cried Vikus, as Luxa, Henry, and Mareth sprang up, swords in hand. "Stay you!"

The rat regarded the three armed humans with amusement. "Yes, stay you or I shall be forced to move, and that always puts me in an ill humor," he said languidly.

Luxa and Mareth stopped uncertainly, but Henry ignored Vikus's command and lunged at the rat. Without moving another muscle, the rat flicked his tail. It cracked like a whip knocking the sword from Henry's hand. The blade spun across the stone floor and slammed into the cavern wall. Henry gripped his wrist in pain.

"The hardest lesson for a soldier to learn is to obey orders he believes are wrong," said the rat philosophically. "Take care, lad, or you shall end up like me, stripped of any respectable rank and warming your shabby old hide at the fire of your enemies." The rat nodded at the old man. "Vikus."

"Ripred," said Vikus with a smile. "We have just commenced dining. Will you join us?"

"I thought you'd never ask," said Ripred, pushing himself off the wall and slouching over to the fire. He squatted back on his haunches next to Solovet. "My dear Solovet, how kind of you to fly out to greet me. And with a war on, too."

"I could scarcely have missed an opportunity to break bread with you, Ripred," said Solovet.

"Oh, come now, you know perfectly well you only tagged along to wheedle information out of me," said Ripred. "And to gloat over your victory at the Flames."

"I destroyed you," said Solovet with glee. "Your army turned tail and ran howling into the river."

"Army," snorted Ripred. "Why, they were as much an army as I am a butterfly. I'd have stood a better chance fighting with crawlers." The rat looked at Temp and Tick, who were cowering against the wall, and sighed. "Present company excepted, of course."

Boots frowned and toddled over to Ripred. She pointed her chubby finger up at him. "You mouse?"

"Yes, I'm a mouse. Squeak, squeak. Now shoo-shoo back to your little bug friends," said Ripred, picking up a hunk of dried beef. He tore off a piece with his teeth and noticed Boots hadn't moved. He pulled back his lips to reveal a row of jagged teeth and gave her a sharp hiss.

"Oh!" said Boots, scurrying to her roaches. "Oh!"

"Don't do that," said Gregor. The rat turned his glowing

eyes on him, and Gregor was shocked by what he saw there. The intelligence, the deadliness, and, most surprisingly, the pain. This rat was not like Fangor and Shed. He was much more complicated and much more dangerous. For the first time in the Underland, Gregor felt completely out of his league. If he fought this rat, he wouldn't stand a chance. He would lose. He would be dead.

"Ah, this must be our warrior," said Ripred softly. "How very like your daddy you are."

"Don't scare my sister," said Gregor, trying to keep his voice steady. "She's only a baby."

"From what I hear, she's got more guts than the lot of you combined," said Ripred. "Of course, courage only counts when you can count. I'm presuming the rest of you can count, and will be screwing your courage to the sticking place any minute now."

The rat glanced around at Luxa, Mareth, and Henry, who were keeping their distance. The bats were extending and folding their wings, unsure of what to do. "Well, come on, then, isn't anyone else hungry? I hate dining alone. It makes me feel so unloved."

"I did not prepare them, Ripred," said Vikus.

"Clearly," said the rat. "Clearly my arrival is an unexpected pleasure." He went to work on his beef bone, making an awful scraping sound.

"Meet you, Ripred the gnawer," said Vikus to the group. "He shall be joining the quest as your guide."

There was a quick breathy sound, as half of those gathered inhaled sharply. A long pause followed in which no one exhaled. Gregor tried to make sense of what Vikus had announced so calmly. A rat. He was leaving them in the hands of a rat. Gregor wanted to object, but his throat had frozen.

Finally Luxa spoke up in a voice hoarse with hatred. "No, he shall not. We do not travel with rats."

"'The Prophecy of Gray' requires it, Luxa," said Solovet. "One gnawer beside."

"'Beside' could mean anything," snarled Henry. "Perhaps we leave the gnawer dead 'beside' us."

"Perhaps you do. But having witnessed your last attack, I doubt it," said Ripred, starting on a wedge of cheese.

"We have killed five rats since midday," said Luxa.

"You mean the idiots that I handpicked for cowardice and ineptitude? Oh, yes, bravo, Your Highness. That was a masterly piece of combat," said Ripred, his voice dripping with sarcasm. "Do not flatter yourself you have yet fought a rat."

"They themselves killed Fangor and Shed," said Mareth bravely.

"Well, then, I stand corrected. Fangor and Shed were excellent fighters, on the rare occasions they were sober," said Ripred. "However, I expect they were outnumbered and somewhat thrown by the arrival of our warrior. What say you, Warrior? Do you refuse to go with me as well?"

Gregor looked into Ripred's mocking, tortured eyes. He wanted to refuse, but if he did, could he ever find his dad?

As if following his thoughts, Vikus spoke up. "You need Ripred to guide you to your father. These tunnels are unmapped by humans. You would never find your way without him."

Still, he was a rat. Gregor had only been in the Underland a few days and he already despised rats. They had killed Luxa's and Henry's parents, imprisoned his father, and almost eaten him and Boots. He felt a kind of power surging through him when he thought of how much he hated them. But if all rats were bad, who was this strange creature staring at him from across the fire, offering to be their guide?

"So, what's in this for you?" said Gregor to Ripred.

"A fair question," said Ripred. "Well, Warrior, I am planning to overthrow King Gorger and I need you to help me."

"By doing what?" said Gregor.

"I don't know," admitted Ripred. "None of us does."

Gregor rose and caught Vikus by the arm. "I have to talk to you alone," he said. The anger in his voice surprised even himself. Well, he *was* angry! The rat was not part of what he'd agreed to. This was not what he'd signed on for.

Vikus took Gregor's mood in stride. Maybe he had expected it. They walked about twenty yards away from the group. "So, how long have you had this plan with the rat?" asked Gregor.

Vikus thought a moment. "I am not sure exactly. Perhaps two or so years. Of course, it was all dependent upon your arrival."

"How come you didn't tell me about it before?" demanded Gregor.

"I do not believe in giving people more information than they can handle," said Vikus.

"Who says I can't handle it? I can handle it!" said Gregor, obviously not handling it.

"Perhaps you can, at least more easily than Luxa and Henry. I may well have told you if we had ever finished our discussion of 'The Prophecy of Gray,'" said Vikus. "No doubt you would have asked, and, yes, I may well have told you."

Gregor pulled the prophecy from his pocket and said, "Let's finish it now." He searched out the part of the prophecy where they'd left off.

ONE GNAWER BESIDE AND ONE LOST UP AHEAD.

"So Ripred is the 'gnawer,' and my dad is the 'one lost up ahead,'" said Gregor. He read on.

AND EIGHT WILL BE LEFT WHEN WE COUNT UP THE DEAD.

"What does that mean?" asked Gregor, pointing to the line.

"If you add up all the players in the prophecy, two over, two under, two fliers, two crawlers, two spinners, one gnawer, and one lost, you have twelve," said Vikus gravely. "By the end of the quest, only eight will remain alive. Four will be dead. But no one knows what four."

"Oh," said Gregor, stunned. He'd heard the words before, but they only registered now. "Four of us dead."

"But eight alive, Gregor," said Vikus gently. "And perhaps a world saved."

Gregor couldn't deal with that part now, wondering who would be left standing at the end of the day. He pushed on to the final stanza of the prophecy.

THE LAST WHO WILL DIE MUST DECIDE WHERE HE STANDS.
THE FATE OF THE EIGHT IS CONTAINED IN HIS HANDS.
SO BID HIM TAKE CARE, BID HIM LOOK WHERE HE LEAPS,
AS LIFE MAY BE DEATH AND DEATH LIFE AGAIN REAPS.

"I don't get this last part," said Gregor.

"Nor do I, nor does anyone. It is very cryptic. I believe no one will fully understand it until the final moment has arrived," said Vikus. "Gregor, it is not pleasant, it is not easy, but it is essential, what I ask you to do. Essential to you, if you wish to find your father. Essential for my people, if they are to survive."

Gregor felt his anger ebbing and fear filling the empty spaces it left. He took another tack. "I don't want to go with that rat," said Gregor, almost pleading. "He'll kill us."

"No, you cannot judge Ripred by what you know of other rats. He has wisdom unique in any creature. Things were not always so bad between humans and rats. When Solovet and Ripred and I were younger, we lived in relative peace. Ripred would see that restored, but King Gorger wishes all humans dead," said Vikus.

"So, you're saying Ripred's a good rat," said Gregor, choking on the words.

"If he were not, would I trust my granddaughter to his care?" asked Vikus.

"Your granddaughter?" said Gregor blankly.

"Luxa's mother was my daughter, Judith," said Vikus.

"You're her grandpa? Why does she call you Vikus?" asked Gregor. These people were so weird and formal. How could he not have known that?

"It is our way," said Vikus. "Look after her. If this is hard for you, know it is torture for Luxa."

"I haven't said I'm going yet!" said Gregor. He looked into the old man's eyes. "All right, I'm going. Is there anything else I need to know that you haven't told me?"

"Only this: Despite what I said, I knew you were the warrior from the first moment I spied you," said Vikus.

"Thanks. Great. That's very helpful," said Gregor, and they returned to the group. "Okay, Boots and I are going with the rat. Who else is in?"

There was a pause. "Where goes the princess, go we," said Temp.

"What say you, Luxa?" said Vikus.

"What can I say, Vikus? Can I return to our people and tell them I withdrew from the quest when our survival hangs in the balance?" said Luxa bitterly.

"Of course you cannot, Luxa. This is why he times it so," said Henry.

"You could choose to —" started Vikus.

"I could choose! I could choose!" retorted Luxa. "Do not offer me a choice when you know none exists!" She and Henry turned their backs on Vikus.

"Fliers?" said Solovet, as Vikus seemed to have lost the ability to talk.

"Aurora and I go with our bonds," muttered Ares.

"Then it is settled. Come, Mareth, we are needed at home," said Solovet.

A distraught Mareth quickly made up packs of food for the members of the quest. "Fly you high, all of you," he said in a strained voice, and climbed on his bat.

Solovet mounted her bat and unrolled her map. While Ripred helped her work out the safest route back to Regalia, Vikus moved to Henry and Luxa. Neither of them would turn to look at him.

"I would not part this way, but I understand your hearts. Perhaps one day you will be able to forgive me this moment. Fly you high, Henry. Fly you high, Luxa," said Vikus. He waited for a response, but none came. He turned and climbed heavily onto his bat.

As miserable as Gregor felt about being dumped with a rat, his heart ached for Vikus. He wanted to scream at Luxa, "Say something! Don't let your grandpa fly off like this! Four of us aren't coming back!" But the words caught in his throat. Part of him wasn't ready to forgive Vikus for abandoning them, either.

"Fly you high, Gregor the Overlander," said Vikus.

Gregor struggled with how to respond. Should he ignore Vikus? Let him know that none of them, not even an Overlander, could forgive him? Just as he had steeled himself against replying, Gregor thought of the last two years, seven months, and, was it fifteen days now? There were so many things he wished he'd said to his dad when he'd had the chance. Things like how special it was when they went on the roof at night and tried to find stars. Or how much he loved it when they took the subway out to the stadium to watch a baseball game. Or just that he felt lucky that out of all the people in the world, his dad was his dad.

He didn't have room inside him for any more unspoken words. The bats were rising into the air. He only had a second. "Fly you high, Vikus!" he yelled. "Fly you high!"

Vikus turned back, and Gregor could see tears shining on his cheeks. He lifted up a hand to Gregor in thanks.

And then they were gone.

CHAPTER

20

It was just the nine of them then. Gregor felt like all the grown-ups had gone home and left the kids with a rat for a baby-sitter. Inside, he felt sick and hollow and very young. He looked around the group and realized there was no one he could turn to for protection.

"We may as well get some rest," said Ripred with a big yawn. "Start fresh in a few hours." He brushed some cheese crumbs off his fur, curled up in a ball, and was snoring loudly within a minute.

No one else knew what to say. Gregor spread his blanket on the floor and called Boots over.

"Go bye-bye?" asked Boots, pointing in the direction Vikus had departed.

"They went bye-bye, Boots. We're going to sleep here. Beddy-bye time." He lay down on the blanket, and she curled up with him without protest. Temp and Tick positioned themselves on either side of them. Were they standing guard? Did they really think there was anything they could do if Ripred decided to attack them? Still, it was kind of comforting to have them there.

Luxa refused to lie down. Aurora came and wrapped her golden wings around her. Ares pressed his black, furry back against Aurora's, and Henry lay at his feet.

They could take whatever precautions they wanted to, but Gregor felt sure Ripred could kill all eight of them in a flash. "He'll take out Henry and Luxa first, since they're the only two with weapons, and then just pick off the rest of us one by one," thought Gregor. Maybe Ares or Aurora could escape, but the rest of them were sitting ducks. That was the truth, he might as well accept it.

Oddly enough, once he did accept it, Gregor felt more relaxed. He didn't have any choice but to trust Ripred. If he could trust Ripred, then he could go to sleep. So he let himself drift off, trying to push the images of striped spider legs and jagged rat teeth from his brain. What a rotten day it had been.

He awoke with a start to a loud slapping sound. He instinctively crouched over Boots until he realized it was just Ripred smacking his tail against the ground.

"Come on, come on," he growled. "Time to get moving. Feed yourselves and let's go."

Gregor crawled out from under his blanket and waited for Mareth to get the food. Then he remembered that

Mareth was gone. "How do you want to handle this food thing?" he asked Henry.

"Luxa and I do not serve food, we are royalty," said Henry haughtily.

"Yeah, well, I'm the warrior and Boots is a princess. And you two are going to get pretty hungry if you're waiting for me to serve you," said Gregor. He was way over this royalty thing.

Ripred laughed. "Tell him, boy. Tell him your country fought a war so you wouldn't have to answer to kings and queens."

Gregor looked at Ripred in surprise. "How do you know that?"

"Oh, I know a great many things about the Overland that our friends here do not. I have spent much time there among your books and papers," said Ripred.

"You can read?" asked Gregor.

"Most rats read. Our frustration is, we cannot hold a pen to write. Now move, Overlander. Eat, don't eat, but let's go," ordered Ripred.

Gregor went to the packs of food to check out the supplies. It was mostly smoked meat, bread, and those sweet potato things. He guessed they might have enough food for three days, if they were careful. Of course, Ripred ate like a pig, and he would probably expect them to feed him. Okay, maybe two days.

Luxa came over and sat awkwardly at his side.

"What?" Gregor said.

"How do we . . . make the food?" she asked.

"What do you mean?" he asked.

"Henry and I, we have never actually prepared food," admitted Luxa.

Gregor could see Henry scowling at Luxa, but she did not look at him.

"You mean, you never even made yourself a sandwich?" asked Gregor. He couldn't cook much, but if his mom had to work late, he'd make dinner sometimes. Just stuff like scrambled eggs or macaroni and cheese, but he could get by.

"A sandwich? Is this a dish named in honor of Bartholomew of Sandwich?" she asked, puzzled.

Gregor said, "I don't really know. It's two slices of bread with meat or cheese or peanut butter or something between them."

"I have not made a sandwich," said Luxa.

"It's not hard. Here, slice off some pieces of meat. Not too thick," he said, handing her a knife. Gregor sawed away at the bread, managing to get eighteen slices out of one loaf. Luxa did a pretty good job with the meat, but then, she was used to handling blades. He showed her how to assemble the sandwiches, and she seemed somewhat pleased with her accomplishment. She took four for herself, her cousin, and the bats. Gregor took the other five. It would be asking too much of her to serve Ripred and the roaches.

He roused Boots, and she started right in on her sandwich. Temp and Tick gave polite nods of thanks for theirs. Then Gregor approached Ripred, who was leaning sulkily in the tunnel. He held out a sandwich. "Here," he said.

174

"For me?" said Ripred, with exaggerated surprise. "How very thoughtful of you. I'm sure the rest of your party would be happy to see me starve."

"If you starve, I'll never find my dad," said Gregor.

"Quite true," said Ripred, popping the entire sandwich in his mouth. "It's good we have this understanding. Mutual need is a strong bond. Stronger than friendship, stronger than love."

"Do rats love?" said Gregor dryly.

"Oh, yes," said Ripred with a smirk. "We love ourselves very much."

"Figures," thought Gregor. He went and sat with Boots, who was polishing off her sandwich.

"More," said Boots, pointing at Gregor's uneaten sandwich. He was ravenous, but he couldn't let her go hungry. He started to break his sandwich in half when Temp delicately pushed his sandwich in front of Boots.

"The princess may eat mine," said Temp.

"You need to eat, too, Temp," objected Gregor.

"Not much," said Temp. "Tick will share her food with me."

Her food. So Tick must be a girl roach.

"He will share with me," said Tick.

And Temp was a guy. Not that it made any difference to Gregor; it was just one more way he could avoid insulting the bugs.

Since Boots had already munched halfway through Temp's sandwich, Gregor accepted. He'd try to give them part of his food at the next meal.

Breakfast was finished in two minutes, and they packed up. They were starting to mount Ares and Aurora when Ripred stopped them. "Don't bother. You cannot fly where we go," he said, and indicated the tunnel. It was barely six feet high and only a few feet wide.

"We're going in there? Isn't there another way to get to my dad?" asked Gregor. He didn't want to head into the dark, narrow space with Ripred, even if they had mutual need.

"There is another way, but not a better way. Unless you know one," said Ripred.

Gregor could feel Ares and Aurora twitching in distress. "What about the bats?"

"I'm sure you'll work that out," drawled Ripred.

"Can you walk?" Gregor asked Ares.

"Not long. Not far," said Ares.

"Then we'll have to carry you," said Gregor.

"Ride you, fliers, ride you?" asked Temp.

"Fliers do not ride crawlers," said Aurora edgily.

"Why not? They rode on you," said Gregor. He was tired of everybody being snooty to the roaches. They never complained and they pulled their weight and they looked after Boots. All in all, the bugs were the easiest traveling companions.

The bats fluttered but didn't answer. "Well, I'm not carrying you. I've already got Boots and a pack of pot roasts. And Luxa and Henry can't carry you both. So, if you're too good to ride on the crawlers, I guess you'd better ask Ripred for a lift."

"Do not use that tone with them," snapped Luxa. "They do not sneer at the crawlers. It is the smallness of the tunnel. Fliers do not like a place they cannot spread their wings."

"Yeah, well, half of us haven't been having much fun flying hundreds of feet in the air, either," said Gregor. He realized he was beginning to sound like a jerk. Ares and Aurora had not been mean or impatient when he and the roaches were scared of flying. "Look, I know it'll be hard, but I'm sure the whole trip won't be in such small tunnels. Right, Ripred?"

"Oh, surely not the *whole* trip," said Ripred, bored to pieces by the argument. "Can we start, please? The war will be over before we decide our travel plans."

"We will ride with the crawlers," said Ares shortly.

Gregor helped Luxa and Henry set the bats on the roaches' backs. They had to lie facedown and cling to the smooth shells with their claws. Gregor had to admit it looked like an uncomfortable way to travel. He tucked Boots in the backpack and picked up his share of the food. "Okay, lead the way," he said to Ripred.

"Finally," Ripred said, and slid into the black hole of the tunnel. Henry followed next, with a torch and a drawn sword. Gregor guessed he was trying to give the bats some feeling of protection. They went next, single file, on the roaches.

Gregor waited for Luxa to enter the tunnel, but she shook her head. "No, Overlander, I think it best that I cover our backs."

"Probably," said Gregor, realizing he still didn't have a

sword. He went into the tunnel giving Boots the flashlight to hold. Luxa brought up the rear.

It was awful. Cramped and airless, with some foul liquid that smelled like rotten eggs dripping from the ceiling. The bats were stiff with discomfort, but the crawlers seemed at home.

"Ick," said Boots as a drop of liquid landed on Gregor's hard hat. "Icky."

"Yeah, ick, ick, icky," agreed Gregor. He hoped the tunnel wasn't long; you could go crazy pretty fast in here. He turned back to check on Luxa. She didn't look happy, but she was managing.

"What means this 'icky'?" she asked him.

"Um, icky, yucky, gross, nasty . . . foul," said Gregor.

"Yes, that describes well the rats' land," said Luxa with a sniff.

"Hey, Luxa," he said. "How come you were surprised when Ripred showed up? I mean, I don't really know the prophecy, but you do. Didn't you expect a rat?"

"No. I thought 'one gnawer beside' meant a rat would be tracking us, perhaps even chasing us. I never imagined he would be part of the quest," she said.

"Vikus said we can trust him," said Gregor.

"Vikus says many things," said Luxa. She sounded so angry that Gregor decided to let the conversation drop.

They trudged on for a while in silence. From the periodic splashes on his face, Gregor knew that Boots must be getting wet. He tried to put his hard hat on her, but it kept slipping off. Finally he dug out some catch cloths and tied them on Boots's head. The last thing they needed was for her to catch a cold.

After several dismal hours, everyone was soaked and miserable. Ripred led them into a small cavern. The smelly water ran down along the sides of the place like rain. The bats were so stiff that Luxa and Henry had to lift them off the roaches and help straighten out their wings.

Ripred lifted his nose in the air and took a deep sniff. "There. That has done much to conceal your odor," he said with satisfaction.

"You mean you just took us that way so we'd all smell like rotten eggs?" said Gregor.

"Quite necessary. As a pack, you were highly repugnant," said Ripred.

Gregor was too worn out to argue. He and Luxa opened up the packs and doled out food. No one felt like talking. Ripred swallowed his lunch in a gulp and stood in the entrance to the tunnel.

They were just finishing up when the bats went tense. "Spinners," warned Aurora.

"Yes, yes, they've been on our trail almost since we started our journey. I cannot smell how many in this place, with all the water. What can they want, I wonder?" Ripred flicked his tail at Luxa and Henry and gave an order. "Three-point arc, you two."

Luxa and Henry exchanged a look and didn't move.

"Three-point arc and this is no time to test my authority, pups!" growled Ripred, baring his terrible teeth. Henry and Luxa reluctantly took places on either side of Ripred, but back a few feet. The three formed a small arc between the rest of the party and the tunnel entrance. The bats took positions behind them.

Gregor strained his ears, but all he could hear was the water falling. Was there an army of spiders after them? He felt, as usual, unarmed and defenseless. He didn't even have a root beer this time.

Everyone became motionless. Gregor could tell that Temp and Tick sensed the invaders now, too. Boots solemnly sucked on a cookie, but didn't make a sound.

Gregor could see the muscles rippling in anticipation along Ripred's broad gray back as the spinners approached. He braced himself for a wave of bloodthirsty spiders, but it never came.

A large orange spider with a small brown spider on its back staggered in and collapsed on the floor. The brown one was oozing a strange blue liquid. It made a great effort to sit up. Its front legs brushed its chest as it spoke. "Vikus sends us. Gnawers attacked webs. Many spinners lost. We two . . . we join . . . the quest."

And with that, the brown spider fell over dead.

Gregor looked at the spider in shock. In its final moments, it had rolled onto its back and curled up its legs. Blue liquid seeped out of a wound in its belly staining the stone floor.

"So, we're all here," said Gregor softly.

"What do you mean?" asked Henry.

Gregor pulled the prophecy from his pocket. "Sandwich was right. We're all here together. At least we were for a few seconds." He read aloud:

> "TWO OVER, TWO UNDER, OF ROYAL DESCENT,
> TWO FLIERS, TWO CRAWLERS, TWO SPINNERS ASSENT.
> ONE GNAWER BESIDE AND ONE LOST UP AHEAD."

He couldn't bring himself to say the next line, but Ripred could. "And eight will be left when we count up the dead.

Well, one down and three to go," said Ripred, poking the spider with the end of his tail.

"Stop it!" said Gregor.

"Oh, what? We can't pretend that any of us was very attached to this spinner. We don't even know its name. Except maybe you," Ripred said to the orange spider.

"Treflex," said the orange spider. "I am she called Gox."

"Well, Gox, I suppose you're hungry after your journey, but our food is limited. None of us will think less of you if you'd like to dine on Treflex," said Ripred.

Gox immediately began to pump juice into Treflex.

"She's not going to — oh, man!" said Gregor.

"Spiders are neither squeamish nor sentimental," said Ripred. "Thank goodness for that."

Gregor turned away so neither he nor Boots had to watch the cannibalism. He was glad to see that Henry and Luxa looked a little green, too.

"Look, if anything happens to me or Boots, don't let that spinner drink us. Toss us off the cliff, in a river, anything, okay?" he said.

They both nodded. "You will return the same favor for us?" said Luxa wanly. "And our bats?"

"And Tick and Temp, too. I promise," said Gregor. He could hear the slow sucking sounds as Gox drained Treflex's body. "Geez," he added.

Fortunately it didn't take Gox long to eat. Ripred began to grill her about the rat attack. She told him an entire army — several hundred rats, at least — had invaded the land of the spiders. The spiders had held them off, but many had died on both sides before the rats had finally retreated. Vikus had come by after the carnage and had sent Gox and Treflex on his bat to the tunnel entrance. "Why?" asked Gox. "Why do the gnawers kill us?"

"I don't know. It may be that King Gorger has launched a total Underland attack. Or it may be they caught wind of two Overlanders heading toward our land. Did they mention the warrior of 'The Prophecy of Gray'?" asked Ripred.

"There were no words, only death," said Gox.

"It is quite fortunate you found us. It would have taken much time to free two spinners from King Gorger's prisons unnoticed, and we have no time to waste," said Ripred to Gox. He turned to Gregor. "This attack on the spinners does not bode well for your father."

"Why? What? Why not?" asked Gregor, feeling his insides go icy.

"Vikus has done a remarkable job of concealing you. No rat save me has seen you and lived to tell of it. The rats do not know the warrior has arrived. But the fact that humans have brought Overlanders to the spinners will make them suspicious," said Ripred. The wheels seemed to be visibly turning in his head. "Still, there is much confusion in war and no rat has identified you. We move on now!"

No one argued. They packed up and headed out the far side of the cavern into a drier, roomier tunnel. Aurora and Ares were able to fly now, although the space was dangerous for riders.

"We shall go on foot," Luxa told Aurora. "Even if you carry the rest of us, what will be done with the gnawer?" So, the bats took to the air with the remaining packs.

Gregor watched them enviously. "Lucky I'm not a bat. I might just fly out of here and not look back."

"Aurora and Ares would never do that. They are bonded to myself and Henry," said Luxa.

"How does that work exactly?" asked Gregor.

"When a bat and a human bond, they swear to fight to the death for each other," said Luxa. "Aurora would never leave me in danger, nor I her."

"Does everybody have a bat?" asked Gregor, thinking it would be nice to know somebody was going to hang around and defend you in this place.

"Oh, no. Some never find a bat to bond with. I became one with Aurora when I was quite young, but this is not common," said Luxa.

"How come you bonded so early?" asked Gregor.

"After my parents were killed, I went through a time where I never felt safe on the ground. I spent all my waking hours in the air on Aurora. It is why we fly so well together," she said simply. "Vikus convinced the council to allow us to bond early. After that I was not so afraid."

"Are you afraid now?" said Gregor.

"At times," she admitted. "But it is no worse than if I were in Regalia. You see, I tired of constant fear, so I made a decision. Every day when I wake I tell myself that it will be my last. If you are not trying to hold on to time, you are not so afraid of losing it."

Gregor thought this was the single saddest thing anyone had ever said to him. He couldn't answer.

"And then, if you make it to bedtime, you feel the joy of cheating death out of one more day," she said. "Do you see?"

"I think so," said Gregor numbly. An awful thought struck him. Wasn't Luxa's strategy just an extreme form of his own rule? True, he didn't think about dying every day, but he denied himself the luxury of thinking about the future with or without his dad. If he hadn't fallen through the grate in his laundry room and discovered his dad was still alive, if his dad had never come home, how long would he have gone on refusing to be happy? His whole life? "Maybe," he thought. "Maybe my whole life." Gregor hurried on with the conversation.

"So, how do you actually bond with a bat?" he asked Luxa.

"It is a simple ceremony. Many bats and humans gather. You stand face-to-face with your bat and say a vow. Like so," said Luxa, extending her hand and reciting a poem.

> *"Aurora the flier, I bond to you,*
> *Our life and death are one, we two.*
> *In dark, in flame, in war, in strife*
> *I save you as I save my life."*

"And then your bat recites it back, but using your name. Then there is a feast," concluded Luxa.

"So what happens if one of you breaks the vow? Like if Aurora flew off and left you in danger," asked Gregor.

"Aurora would not, but a few vows have been broken. The punishment is severe. The one at fault is banished to live alone in the Underland," said Luxa. "And no one lives long in the Underland alone."

"Fascinating as your native rituals are, do you think we might proceed in silence? Given that the entire rat nation is on the lookout for us, it might be prudent," said Ripred.

Luxa and Gregor shut up. Gregor wished they could talk more. Luxa acted differently when she wasn't with Henry. Friendlier. Less arrogant. But Ripred was right about the noise.

Fortunately Boots dozed off. For several hours all they heard were the light tap of their footsteps and the scraping sound of Ripred's teeth on a bone he'd saved from lunch.

Gregor felt consumed with new worries about his dad. From what Ripred had said, it seemed like the rats might kill him to keep Gregor from reaching him. But why? That wouldn't change the prophecy, would it? He guessed no one really knew. And what about that last stanza? He unrolled the prophecy and read it so many times, he memorized it without trying.

THE LAST WHO WILL DIE MUST DECIDE WHERE HE STANDS.
THE FATE OF THE EIGHT IS CONTAINED IN HIS HANDS.
SO BID HIM TAKE CARE, BID HIM LOOK WHERE HE LEAPS,
AS LIFE MAY BE DEATH AND DEATH LIFE AGAIN REAPS.

He couldn't make heads or tails of it. All he could figure out was that whoever died fourth had a pretty big responsibility to the eight who were still living. But how? What? Where? When? The final stanza of "The Prophecy of Gray" left out all the details that would have made it useful.

Ripred kept them moving until everyone was stumbling with fatigue. He gave the order to stop in a cavern that at least had a dry floor and a spring with drinkable water.

Gregor and Luxa passed around their dwindling food, which was disappearing much faster than he had anticipated. He tried to object when the roaches gave their food to Boots, thinking he would share his own.

"Let them feed her," said Ripred. "A crawler can live a month with no food if it has water. And don't bother feeding Gox. Treflex will hold her for longer than our journey will last."

The cavern was cold. Gregor stripped off Boots's damp clothes and put on a fresh set. Something was wrong with her; she seemed too quiet, and her skin was clammy and cold. He curled up under the blanket with her, trying to warm her up. What would he do if she got sick? They needed to be home with his mom, who always knew just the combination of juice and medicine and pillows to make it all right. He tried to console himself with the idea that his dad could help when they found him.

Everyone was so tired from their trek that they fell asleep immediately.

Something woke Gregor from a heavy sleep. A sound? A

movement? He wasn't sure. All he knew was that when he opened his eyes, Henry was standing over Ripred, ready to plunge his sword into the sleeping rat's back.

CHAPTER

22

Gregor opened his mouth to scream "No!" just as Ripred's eyes flickered. Henry was behind the rat. All Ripred could have seen was the expression on Gregor's face, but it was enough.

In the split second Henry drove the blade down, Ripred flipped onto his back and slashed his terrible claws. The sword cut across the rat's chest as Ripred tore a deep gash along Henry's arm.

About this time, Gregor's "No!" had actually left his mouth, and his yell woke up most of the party. Ripred rose up on his hind legs, bleeding, furious, and terrifying to see. Henry looked weak and small by comparison; he could barely lift his sword with his injured arm. Luxa and Aurora were instantly airborne. Ares flew straight for the rat.

But Gregor got there first. He sprang between Ripred

and Henry with his arms spread out. "Stop!" he cried. "Stop!"

Unbelievably, everyone paused. Gregor guessed this was the first time any of them had ever seen someone try to come between a fighting rat and a human. Their second of hesitation gave him just enough time to blurt out, "Anybody who wants to kill anybody else has to go through me first!"

Not particularly poetic, but it had the desired effect. No one wanted Gregor dead. Everyone knew the warrior was essential to the quest.

"Move, Overlander, the rat will kill us all!" ordered Luxa, preparing to dive at Ripred.

"The rat was merely trying to sleep. Believe me, pup, if I had wanted to kill you we would not be having this conversation," said Ripred.

"Do not waste your lies on us, Gnawer!" said Luxa. "Do you think we would believe your word over one of our own?"

"It's true! He's telling the truth! He didn't start it! It was Henry!" Gregor shouted. "He was trying to kill Ripred in his sleep!"

Everyone turned to Henry, who spat back at them, "Yes, and he would be dead now were it not for the Overlander!"

Now there was confusion. Gregor could tell by the look on Luxa's face she hadn't known about Henry's plan. She'd assumed Ripred had attacked first. She didn't know what to do next.

"Stop, Luxa! Please!" said Gregor. "We can't afford to lose any more questers here! We have to stick together!"

He'd made up the word "questers" on the spot, and it seemed right.

Luxa slowly descended to the ground, but stayed on Aurora's back. Ares hovered uncertainly in the air. Gregor wondered if the bat had known about Henry's plan. But if he had, why hadn't they attacked together from the air? It was so hard to tell what the bats were thinking.

Gregor noticed for the first time that Temp and Tick were literally standing over the sleeping Boots, shielding her. Gox still perched in the makeshift web she'd built at bedtime.

"It's over," Gregor said with an authority he didn't know he possessed. "Put down your sword, Henry. Ripred, just — just sit down! It's over!"

Would they listen to him? Gregor didn't know, but he was determined to hold his ground. It was a long, tense moment. Then Ripred lowered his lips back over his bared fangs and broke into a laugh. "I will say this for you, Warrior, you do not lack boldness."

Henry let his sword clatter to the ground, which was no big concession since Gregor saw he could barely hold it. "Or treachery," said Henry softly.

Gregor narrowed his eyes at Henry. "You know, where I come from, we don't think much of someone who sneaks up and stabs a person in their sleep."

"He is not a person, he is a rat," said Henry. "If you cannot make the distinction, you may surely count yourself among the dead."

Gregor held Henry's cold gaze. He knew that later he

would think of several tough things he should have said to Henry, but he couldn't think of any now. Instead, he turned to Luxa and said gruffly, "We'd better patch them up."

They weren't much better at first aid than they were at cooking, but Luxa at least knew what ointment to use. Gox turned out to be the biggest help of all. She spun a special web and instructed them to press handfuls of the silky threads into the injuries. In minutes, the bleeding on both Henry's arm and Ripred's chest had stopped.

While Gregor patted extra layers of silk onto Ripred's matted fur, the rat muttered, "I suppose I ought to thank you."

"Forget about it," said Gregor. "I only did it because I need you." He didn't want Ripred thinking they were friends or anything.

"Did you? I'm glad," said Ripred. "I thought I detected in you a sense of fair play. Most dangerous in the Underland, boy."

Gregor wished everybody would just shut up about what was dangerous to him in the Underland. The whole place was one big minefield. He ignored Ripred's comment and continued to apply the spiderwebs. Behind him he heard Luxa whisper to Henry, "Why did you not tell us?"

"To keep you safe," Henry whispered back.

"Safe," thought Gregor. "Right." Even if he got back to the Overland, Gregor didn't think he would ever feel safe again.

"You must not do this again, Henry," he heard Luxa say. "You cannot take him alone."

"I could have, if the Overlander had not interfered," said Henry.

"No, the risk is too great, and we may have need of him," said Luxa. "Let the rat be."

"Is that an order, Your Highness?" asked Henry with a slight edge to his voice.

"If that is the only way you will heed my advice, then yes," said Luxa earnestly. "Hold your sword until we better understand our condition."

"You speak most exactly like that old fool Vikus," said Henry.

"No, I speak as myself," said Luxa, stung. "And as one who wishes us both to survive."

The cousins realized their voices had risen to the point where everyone could hear them, so they stopped talking. In the silence, Ripred resumed gnawing on the bone he'd been carrying around. The scraping grated on Gregor's nerves. "Do you think you could stop that, please?" he asked.

"No, actually I can't," said Ripred. "Rats' teeth continue to grow our entire lives, which necessitates gnawing to keep them at a manageable length. If I didn't gnaw frequently, my lower teeth would soon grow through the top of my skull and puncture my brain and alas, kill me."

"Glad I asked," said Gregor, slapping a last piece of web on Ripred and leaning back against the cavern wall. "So, now what?"

"Well, since obviously no one's going back to dreamland, we may as well make tracks for your father," said Ripred, rising to his feet.

Gregor went to get Boots. As soon as he touched her he felt alarmed. Her face was burning like a furnace. "Oh, no," he said helplessly. "Hey, Boots. Hey, little girl." He gently shook her shoulder. She whimpered something in her sleep but didn't wake up. "Luxa, something's wrong. Boots is sick," he said.

Luxa laid her hand on Boots's forehead. "She is fevered. She has caught some pestilence from the land of rats." Pestilence. Gregor hoped that wasn't as serious as it sounded. Luxa dug through the vials Solovet had left with them and held one up uncertainly. "I think this is for fever."

Ripred took a sniff and wrinkled his nose. "No, that kills pain." He buried his snout in the pack and rooted out a blue glass bottle. "You need this one. Give her only a few drops. She cannot handle more at her size."

Gregor was reluctant to give her any of the strange medicine, but Boots was so hot. He slipped a few drops between her lips and thought she swallowed it. He tried to lift her up to put her in the pack, and she moaned in pain. He bit his lip. "She can't ride with me; it hurts her."

They laid Boots on a blanket on Temp's back. Gox spun a web to secure her to the shell.

Gregor felt sick with worry.

AND EIGHT WILL BE LEFT WHEN WE COUNT UP THE DEAD.

He couldn't lose Boots. He just couldn't. He had to get her home. He should have left her in Regalia. He should never have agreed to the quest. If anything happened to Boots, it would be his fault.

The gloom of the tunnel soaked through his skin and into his veins. He wanted to scream out in pain, but the darkness choked him. He would have given almost anything for just one glimpse of the sun.

The party limped along slowly, painfully, suspiciously, preoccupied by the worries they all shared, but no one spoke aloud. Even Ripred, by far the most hardened of the group, seemed to hunch down under the weight of the situation.

This general despair was just one of the reasons they didn't detect the score of rats until they were almost on top of them. Even Ripred could not distinguish the smell of rats in a place reeking of rats. The bats couldn't sense them in the narrow tunnel as they approached the increasingly loud river. The humans could see nothing in the gloom.

Ripred led them out of the tunnel into a huge cavern divided by a deep canyon. A wide, powerful river ran through it. A swinging bridge spanned the river. It must have been made with the combined efforts of several species in better times. Thick silk woven by the spiders supported thin slats of stone cut by the humans. They must have needed the bats' flying abilities, too, to build such a bridge.

When Gregor shone his flashlight up to see how the bridge was secured, he caught sight of them. Twenty rats sitting motionless on the rocks above the opening to the tunnel. Right above their heads. Waiting.

"Run!" Ripred yelled, and literally snapped his teeth at Gregor's heels. Gregor stumbled forward onto the bridge and began to cross, his feet slipping on the worn stone slats. He could feel Ripred's hot breath on his neck. Henry and Luxa were flying ahead of him, jetting across the river.

He was halfway across when he remembered Boots wasn't on his back. She had been with him so continually on the journey, he had begun to think of them as inseparable. But now she was on Temp!

Gregor turned abruptly to go back. Ripred, as if anticipating just this move, spun Gregor forward and snagged the backpack with his teeth. Gregor felt himself lifted into the air as Ripred ran flat out for the far side of the river.

"Boots!" yelled Gregor. "Boots!"

Ripred moved like lightning. As he reached the opposite bank, he dumped Gregor on the ground and joined Luxa and Henry, who were frantically trying to hack through the silk ropes supporting the bridge.

Gregor aimed his flashlight and saw that Gox was about three quarters of the way across. Behind her, carrying his sister, Temp struggled along with Boots. Between Boots and the twenty killer rats that were now streaming across the bridge — there was only Tick.

"Boots!" Gregor screamed, and dove back for the bridge. Ripred's tail caught him across the chest and flung him back onto the ground, knocking the wind from him. He gasped, trying to fill his lungs, then got to his knees and crawled toward the bridge. He had to help her. He had to.

Gox zipped off the bridge and began to snap threads with her jaws. "No!" coughed Gregor. "My sister!" He pulled up to his feet just in time to catch another blow from Ripred's tail.

The roaches were within ten feet of the bank when the rats caught up with them. There was no discussion between them; it was as if the bugs had worked out this whole scenario long ago. Temp put on a burst of speed for the end of the bridge, and Tick turned to face down the army of rats alone.

As they bounded at her, Tick flew directly into the face of the lead rat, causing it to startle back in surprise. Until that moment, Gregor hadn't even realized the roaches had wings. Maybe the rats didn't know, either. But it didn't take them long to recover. The lead rat sprang forward and crushed Tick's head in its jaws.

Temp collapsed on the bank just as the bridge gave way. Twenty rats, the leader still holding Tick in its teeth, plunged into the river below. As if this sight wasn't horrific enough, the water churned as enormous piranha-like fish surfaced and fed on the screaming rats.

In a minute it was all over. The water ran smoothly. The rats had vanished. And Tick was gone forever.

CHAPTER

23

"Move it, move it, move it!" instructed Ripred, herding them all from the open bank and into a tunnel. He forced them along for a few minutes until they were well out of sight and, hopefully, out of smell of the tunnel entrance. At a small chamber, he gave the order to halt. "Stop you. Sit you. Slow your hearts."

Wordlessly, the remaining members of the quest sunk to the floor of the tunnel. Gregor sat with Temp, his back to the others. He pawed up Temp's back, found Boots's hot little fingers, and entwined them with his own. He had almost lost her. Lost her for good. She would never have had the chance to meet their dad or get back to his mom's arms or play in the sprinkler with him and Lizzie or do anything ever again.

He did not want to look at the rest of the questers. Every

one of them would have watched Boots and the crawlers fall into the river to stop the rats. He had nothing to say to them.

And then there was Tick. Brave little Tick, who had flown into the face of an army of rats to save his baby sister. Tick — who never spoke much. Tick — who shared her food. Tick — who was after all just a roach. Just a roach who had given all the time she had left so that Boots could have more.

Gregor pressed Boots's fingers against his lips and felt scalding tears begin to slide down his cheeks. He hadn't cried, not the whole time he'd been down here, and there had been plenty of bad stuff. But somehow Tick's sacrifice had crushed whatever thin shell remained between him and sorrow. From now on, he felt an allegiance to the roaches that he knew would never fade. He would never again take a roach's life. Not here and not — if by some miracle they made it home — in the Overland.

He felt his shoulders began to shake. Probably the others thought he was ridiculous, crying over a roach, but he didn't care. He hated them. He hated them all.

Temp, whose antennas had drooped down over his head, reached out and touched Gregor with a feeler. "Thank you. To weep when Tick has lost time."

"Boots would weep, too, if she weren't . . ." Gregor couldn't go on as another wave of sobs swept over him. He was glad Boots hadn't witnessed Tick's death. She would have been upset and she wouldn't have understood it. He didn't really understand it, either.

Gregor felt a hand on his shoulder and jerked away. He knew it was Luxa, but he didn't want to talk to her. "Gregor," she whispered sadly. "Gregor, know you we would have caught Boots and Temp if they fell. We would have caught Tick, too, had there been any reason."

He pressed his hand against his eyes to stop his tears, and nodded. Well, at least that was a little better. Of course Luxa would have dived after Boots if she'd fallen. The Underlanders didn't worry about falling the way he did, not with their bats.

"It's okay," he said. "I know." When Luxa sat beside him, he didn't move away. "I guess you think it's pretty stupid, me crying over a roach."

"You do not yet know the Underlanders if you think we lack tears," said Luxa. "We weep. We weep, and not just for ourselves."

"Not for Tick, though," said Gregor with a trace of bitterness.

"I have not wept since the death of my parents," said Luxa quietly. "But I am thought to be unnatural in this respect."

Gregor felt more tears slipping down his cheeks when he thought of how badly you had to be hurt to lose the ability to cry. He forgave Luxa everything at that moment. He even forgot why he needed to forgive her.

"Gregor," she said softly when his tears had stopped. "If you return to Regalia, and I do not . . . tell Vikus that I understood."

"Understood what?" asked Gregor.

"Why he left us with Ripred," said Luxa. "We had to have a gnawer. I see now he was trying to protect us."

"Okay, I'll tell him," said Gregor, wiping his nose. He was quiet for a minute, and then he asked, "So, how often do we give Boots that medicine? She still feels pretty hot."

"Let us dose her now, before we move on," said Luxa, stroking Boots's forehead. Boots murmured in her sleep but didn't wake up. They slipped a few more drops from the bottle between her lips. Gregor stood up and tried to shake off the pain. "Let's get going," he said, not looking at Ripred. The rat had been in tons of wars. He'd probably seen lots of creatures killed. He'd told Gox to eat Treflex. Gregor was sure Tick's death affected him as little as . . . well, as swatting a roach affected people in New York.

But when Ripred spoke, his voice lacked its usual snide tone. "Take heart, Overlander. Your father is nearby."

Gregor lifted his head at the words. "How nearby?"

"An hour's walk, no more," said Ripred. "But so are his guards. We must all proceed with extreme caution. Bind your feet in webs, speak not, and stay close behind me. We had rare luck at the bridge. I do not think it follows us where now we go."

Gox, whom Gregor was beginning to appreciate more as time passed, quickly spun thick silk slippers to pad their feet. As Gregor held his flashlight for Luxa to put on her pair, the light faded. He dug in his pack and came up with the last two batteries.

"How much longer can your torchlight last?" Gregor asked Luxa. He had noticed they'd gone to one torch when they met up with Ripred, apparently to conserve fuel. Now the one torch burned low.

"A short time only," admitted Luxa. "Your light stick?"

"I don't know," said Gregor. "These are my last batteries, and I don't know how much power's left in them."

"Once we have your father, we will not need light. Ares and Aurora can get us home in the dark," said Luxa encouragingly.

"They're going to have to," said Gregor.

The questers regrouped. Ripred led with Temp and Boots behind him. The tunnel was large enough for Gregor and Gox to walk beside them. Aurora and Ares fluttered along next, making short, silent flights. Henry and Luxa brought up the rear on foot, swords drawn. Ripred gave them a nod and they started off, deep, deep into enemy territory.

They tiptoed along, scarcely daring to breathe. Gregor froze every time a pebble moved beneath his foot, thinking he had triggered another rat assault. He was very afraid, but a new emotion was rising up in him, giving him strength to keep putting one foot in front of the other. It was hope. It flowed through him, insisting that he break his rule. His father was nearby. He would see him soon. If only they could keep moving forward undetected, he would see him soon.

When they had been creeping along for about half an hour, Ripred suddenly stopped at a bend in the tunnel. The whole party pulled up behind him. Ripred's nose twitched furiously and he crouched.

A pair of rats sprang from around the bend. In an

impossible move, Ripred tore out one's throat with his teeth while his back feet blinded the second. In another flash, both rats lay dead. No one else had had time to raise a hand. Ripred's defense confirmed what Gregor had suspected the first moment he'd looked in his eyes. Even among rats, Ripred was lethal.

Ripred wiped his muzzle on one of the dead rats and spoke in a whisper. "Those were the guards to this passage. We are about to enter open space. Stay against the wall, single file, for the earth is unstable and the fall immeasurable." Everyone nodded numbly, still stunned by his ferocity. "It's all right," he added. "Remember, I'm on your side."

Around the bend of the tunnel was the opening.

Ripred made a right turn, and they peeled off in single file behind him. A narrow path led along the side of a canyon. When Gregor shone his light into it, he saw nothing but blackness. "And the fall is immeasurable," he thought.

The ground under his left foot, the one closest to the void, crumbled and sent a shower of stone and dirt into the darkness. Gregor never heard it hit the bottom. His only consolation was that Aurora and Ares were inching along somewhere behind him, ready to save anyone who fell.

After about fifty yards they reached the more solid ground that fanned out from one end of the canyon. A natural arch of stone framed a wide road, worn smooth by many rat feet. Ripred picked up speed as they crossed under the arch, and Gregor felt that any protection the terrain had given them was gone.

Ripred, Temp, Gox, and Gregor raced down the road.

Luxa and Henry had instinctively taken to the air. Gregor felt as if rat eyes must be burning at them from every crevice.

The path ended abruptly at a deep circular pit with walls as smooth as ice. A faint light burned in the pit revealing a furry creature hunched over a stone slab, fiddling with something. At first Gregor raised a warning hand. He thought it was a rat.

Then the creature lifted his head and Gregor recognized what was left of his dad.

CHAPTER

24

The man who had disappeared from Gregor's life two years, seven months, and who knew how many days ago had been the picture of health. Strong, tall, and vibrant, energy had seemed to pour right out of him. The man squinting up at them from the pit was so thin and weak, his attempt to stand failed. He fell on all fours, then lifted one hand to help tilt his own head back.

"Dad?" Gregor tried to say, but all the moisture had left his mouth. He dropped to his own knees at the side of the pit and reached out a hand futilely. They were fifty feet apart, but he reached, anyway.

Luxa and Henry flew down, helped the pitiful form onto Aurora's back, and carried him up.

Still on his knees, Gregor clutched his father's hands, once so strong and capable. As he felt the bones beneath his fingers he remembered how his dad used to crack walnuts with his hands. "Dad?" he said, and this time he could be heard. "Dad, it's me. Gregor."

His father frowned as if trying to remember something. "It's the fever. I'm seeing things again."

"No, Dad, it's me, I'm here. And Boots is here, too," said Gregor.

"Boots?" said his dad. He frowned again, and Gregor remembered he had never seen Boots. She had been born after he fell.

"Margaret," Gregor corrected himself. As soon as his mom was pregnant, his parents had planned to name Boots Margaret after his dad's grandma.

"Margaret?" said his dad, now thoroughly confused. He rubbed his eyes. "Grandma?"

The prophecy had named "one lost up ahead," but Gregor had not expected to find his dad as lost as this. He was skeletal and weak — and what had happened to his hair and beard? They were snow white. Gregor touched his father's shoulder and realized he was wearing a cloak made of rat fur. No wonder he had looked like a rat from above.

"Just want to sleep," said his father vaguely. This was the scariest part of all. Gregor had thought he would get a parent back when he found his dad. Then he could stop having to make hard decisions. He could just be a kid. But the man before him was even needier than Boots was.

Luxa laid her hand on his dad's cheek and frowned. "He burns like your sister, and he has no strength to fight it. This is why he speaks in confusion."

"Maybe if I talk to him a minute, he'll remember. He's got to remember, Luxa," said Gregor desperately.

"We must fly now, Gregor," insisted Luxa, tipping a large swallow from the blue bottle into his dad's mouth. "We shall heal him properly in Regalia. Henry, help me secure him." She tried to tie his dad to Aurora with a length of silk that Gox was rapidly spinning. "Henry?" said Luxa again.

But Henry stood apart from them. Not helping. Not hurrying. Not even bothering to seem anxious. "No, Luxa, we have no need to hurry now."

It was a strange answer. No one understood what he was saying except Ripred. An odd look crossed the rat's face. "No, I believe Henry has taken care of everything."

"Henry had to," said Henry. He lifted his fingers to his lips and gave a long whistle.

"Are you crazy? What are you doing?" asked Gregor. He looked at Luxa, who seemed to have turned to marble. The silk rope slipped from her hands and fell to the ground.

The patter of many rat feet came at them down the road. What was going on? What had Henry done?

"Ripred?" said Gregor.

"It seems I am not the only spy among us, Overlander," said Ripred wryly. "A member of the royal family, too."

"You mean, Henry . . . ?" Gregor would never in a million years have believed Henry to be a spy for the rats. They had killed his parents, his people. "He can't be," blurted out Gregor. "He can't, I mean, what about Luxa?" The two were so tight.

207

"Sorry, cousin," said Henry urgently to Luxa. "But I had no choice. We were headed for disaster under Vikus. He would ally us to the weakest, when our only real chance of survival is to ally ourselves with those who are most powerful. We will join forces with the rats and rule together, you and I."

Luxa spoke more calmly than Gregor had ever heard her. "Not now, Henry. Not ever."

"You must, Luxa, you have no choice. You must join with us or die," said Henry coldly, but there was a tremor in his voice.

"This is as good a day as any," said Luxa. "Perhaps better." She sounded a thousand years old and a thousand miles away, but she did not sound scared.

"So they promised you a throne, did they? Really, Henry, you are not fool enough to believe they will deliver it," said Ripred, breaking into a laugh.

"They will deliver it. Together we will rid the Underland of crawlers and spinners and share their land among us," said Henry.

"But why? Why would you do that?" asked Gregor.

"I am tired of having cowards and weaklings as allies," said Henry. "The rats, at least, are not guilty of that. Together, we will protect each other. Together, we will rule. Together, we will be safe. It has been decided."

"Together, together," said Ripred in a singsong voice. "What a lot of togetherness you are planning. And what a lot of solitude awaits you. Ah, here are your friends now."

There were at least fifty of them. The rats fanned out quickly and circled the questers. Most of them were laughing, delighted at the rich catch before them.

Gregor's eyes darted around. Who would fight on his side? His dad was mumbling something about fish. Boots lay tied to Temp's back, oblivious to the world. Henry was a traitor, so he could count Ares out, too, since the pair was bonded. That left him, Luxa, Aurora, Gox, and . . . suddenly he didn't know what to think of Ripred. What about Ripred? Whose side was the rat really on?

He looked at Ripred, and the rat gave him a slow wink. "Remember, Gregor, the prophecy calls for only four of the twelve to die. Think we can take them, you and I?"

Okay, he also had one amazing rat on his side.

The circle widened, leaving a gap. A huge silver rat strode into the space. Jammed over one ear was a gold crown, clearly designed for a human head. Gregor heard Luxa inhale sharply and guessed it had belonged to one of her parents.

"King Gorger," said Ripred, giving a low bow. "I did not hope we would have the honor of your presence here."

"An unfortunate crawler told us you drowned, Ripred," said the king in a low voice.

"Yes, well, that was the plan," said Ripred, nodding. "But so often plans go awry."

"We must thank you for bringing the warrior so neatly into our paws. It was Henry's job really, but no matter as long as he is here. I wanted to be sure. I wanted to see him for myself before I killed him. So this is he?" asked

King Gorger, peering at Gregor. "I expected so much more."

"Oh, do not judge him too quickly," said Ripred. "I have found him most delightfully full of surprises." He made his way around the circle, occasionally lifting a front leg to scratch his nose. Each time he lifted his paw the rats near him flinched. "Clawsin . . . Bloodlet . . . now break my heart, Razor, is that you? You have no idea how it hurts me to see you in His Majesty's company."

The rat Razor dropped his eyes away from Ripred's. Was he ashamed? Could rats even feel ashamed?

Ripred came up behind Henry and nudged him forward. "Go, go, go, go. Stand with your friends." Henry tripped and fell into place beside King Gorger, stepping on his tail. The other rats laughed, but not the king who whipped his tail out from under Henry and slashed poor Gox in half.

The rats stopped laughing. Gregor saw the spider's blue blood gushing onto the ground. It was that quick. In a split second, a third member of the quest was dead.

"Why has everyone stopped laughing?" said King Gorger. "Go on, laugh!" he ordered, and the rats let out a sound like sheep bleating. He stretched out on the ground in a pose of complete relaxation, but Gregor could see his muscles were still tense with anger.

"Who's next?" said King Gorger. "Come, do not be shy. Shall we take care of the pup? She looks soon to expire, anyway." He trained his ratty eyes on Boots.

"Not Boots," thought Gregor. "Not while I can stand." Something nagged at the back of his brain. What was it?

What did it remind him of? And suddenly he knew. He knew what the next part of the prophecy meant.

THE LAST WHO WILL DIE MUST DECIDE WHERE HE STANDS.
THE FATE OF THE EIGHT IS CONTAINED IN HIS HANDS.

"It's me," he realized. "I'm the last to die." It was clear. It was Gregor the rats wanted. He was the warrior. He was the threat. He was the one who had to decide where he stood. And it wasn't going to be here, watching people he loved die. He was the warrior, and the warrior saved people.

Once he knew, it was easy. He judged the height, ran seven steps, and hurdled over the silver back of King Gorger.

A howl rose up behind him as he flew down the road. From some rat screams that came after that, he guessed Luxa, Aurora, and Ripred had gone into action to cover him. But he was pretty sure that every able-bodied rat was chasing after him. Good. That way, with any luck, the others could escape. Except Henry and Ares — he didn't care what happened to them.

The flashlight in his hand dimmed to a faint glow, and he tossed it off to the side. It was slowing him down, anyway. But running in the dark was no good. He might trip, and he had to lead the rats as far away as possible from everybody. Then he remembered the light on his hat. He had meant to save it as a last resort. If there was ever a last resort, this was it. He flipped on the switch without breaking stride, and the powerful beam lit the road in front of him.

But the road! He had forgotten how short the road was!

No more than a hundred yards ahead of him loomed the canyon, the one of "immeasurable depth." He didn't stand a chance trying to run around the edge of it. The rats would have him in seconds.

He didn't want to die that way. He didn't want to give the rats the satisfaction of eating him. He could hear them behind him, breathing and snapping their teeth. King Gorger snorted in fury.

In one horrible moment the last piece of the prophecy became clear.

SO BID HIM TAKE CARE, BID HIM LOOK WHERE HE LEAPS,
  AS LIFE MAY BE DEATH AND DEATH LIFE AGAIN REAPS.

He had to leap, and by his death, the others would live. That was it. That was what Sandwich had been trying to say all along, and by now he believed Sandwich.

He put on a final burst of speed, just like the coach taught him in track. He gave it everything he had. In the last few steps before the canyon he felt a sharp pain in the back of his leg, and then the ground gave way under his feet.

Gregor the Overlander leaped.

CHAPTER

25

Gregor soared out over the canyon, throwing his body as high into the air as he could get. He could feel warm blood running down his leg. One of the rats had gotten a claw into him just as he was taking off.

"I'm falling," thought Gregor. "Just like when I came to the Underland." Only he was falling much faster now. There was no current supporting him from underneath, just the hideous void gaping below him. He had never really understood how he had landed safely the first time. Never had a moment of quiet and clarity to ask Vikus. Now he guessed he would never know.

Maybe it was all part of the same dream and he would finally wake up in his own bed and he could go and find his mom and tell her all about it. But Gregor knew it wasn't a dream anymore. He was really falling. And when he hit the bottom, he would not wake up in bed.

Something else was different from his first fall. By the sound of it, he had a lot more company.

Gregor managed to twist himself around in the air. The light from his hard hat lit up an astonishing scene. The rats who had been chasing him, and it must have been about all of them, were falling after him in an avalanche of stone. The unstable ground at the edge of the canyon had given way, bringing the whole army down after him.

With shock, Gregor saw a human was among the rats. Henry. He had been chasing Gregor, too. But that couldn't be right. They both couldn't end up dead. The prophecy only called for one more quester to die.

A flash of wing gave Gregor his answer. Of course. It was Ares, the bat who was bonded to this traitor. Ares would save Henry, and the prophecy would be fulfilled. But the rest of the questers would be safe, too.

Gregor had never seen Ares dive in earnest. He was heading for the ground at tremendous speed, dodging the rats that reached for him. Gregor began to doubt he would be able to pull out of it. "He overshot," thought Gregor as the bat rocketed past Henry.

He could hear Henry's desperate plea: "Ares!"

At that moment, Gregor slammed into something.

"I'm dead," he thought, but he didn't feel dead because his nose hurt so badly and his mouth was full of fur. Then he had the sensation of rising and he knew he was on Ares's back. He looked down over the side of the bat's wing and saw the rats beginning to burst apart on the rocks below.

Gregor had been almost at the bottom when Ares had caught him. The sight of the rats was unbearable, even if they had just been about to kill him. Just before Henry hit, Gregor buried his face in Ares's fur and covered his ears.

The next thing he knew, they were on the ground. Luxa had his father strapped on Aurora. Temp bolted onto Ares behind him.

A bloody Ripred stood with three other rats that must have joined him in the final moments. He gave Gregor a bitter smile. "Delightfully full of surprises."

"What will you do, Ripred?" asked Gregor.

"Run, boy. Run like the river. Fly you high, Gregor the Overlander!" said Ripred as he took off down the road.

"Fly you high, Ripred! Fly you high!" shouted Gregor as Ares and Aurora sped over the rat's head.

They flew out over the canyon. Somewhere beneath them lay the bodies of King Gorger, his army of rats, and Henry. The canyon ended, and the bats headed into a large tunnel that twisted and turned every which way.

Now that he was safe, Gregor began to feel the fear of falling into that black void. His whole body began to shake. He pressed his face deep in Ares's neck, although it made his nose throb even more. He heard the bat whisper, "I did not know, Overlander. I swear to you I did not know."

"I believe you," Gregor whispered back. If Ares had known about Henry's plot, Henry would be flying somewhere right now and Gregor would be . . .

The last words of the prophecy came back to him again.

THE LAST WHO WILL DIE MUST DECIDE WHERE HE STANDS.
THE FATE OF THE EIGHT IS CONTAINED IN HIS HANDS.
SO BID HIM TAKE CARE, BID HIM LOOK WHERE HE LEAPS,
AS LIFE MAY BE DEATH AND DEATH LIFE AGAIN REAPS.

So, it was about Henry as well as Gregor. Henry had decided to stand with the rats. That had determined the fate of the other eight questers. He had not taken care where he'd leaped, had not looked at all because he was so caught up in helping the rats. Henry had died because of his decision. Even to the last moments he must have thought Ares would save him. But Ares had chosen to save Gregor.

"Overlander, we have troubles," whispered Ares, interrupting his train of thought.

"Why? What's wrong?" asked Gregor.

"Aurora and I, we do not know which direction leads back to Regalia," said Ares.

"You mean we're lost?" said Gregor. "I thought Luxa said you could get us home in the dark."

"Yes, we can fly in the dark, but we must know which way to fly," said Ares. "This area is uncharted by fliers."

"What does Luxa think we should do?" asked Gregor.

There was a pause. Gregor assumed Ares was communicating with Aurora. Then Ares said, "Luxa cannot speak."

"Luxa is probably in shock," thought Gregor. "After what Henry did to her."

"To complicate matters, Aurora has a torn wing that must soon be mended if we are to continue," Ares added.

Gregor suddenly realized he was in charge. "Okay, look for a safe place to land, all right?"

The twisting tunnel soon opened out over a large river. The source was a magnificent waterfall that poured out of a stone arch and fell a hundred feet to the river below. Above the arch was a natural stone ledge, about ten feet deep. Ares and Aurora coasted over to it and landed. Their riders slid onto the stone.

Gregor hurried over to Luxa, hoping to figure out some kind of game plan, but one look at her told him he was on his own. Her eyes were unfocused, and she trembled like a leaf. "Luxa? Luxa?" he asked. As Aurora had reported, she couldn't say a word. Not sure what else to do, Gregor wrapped her in a blanket.

He turned to Aurora next. Her left wing had a long rip that oozed blood. "I can try to sew that up," said Gregor, not relishing the idea. He could sew a little, buttons and small tears. The idea of taking a needle to her delicate wing worried him.

"Tend to the others first," said Aurora. She fluttered over to Luxa and wrapped her good wing around the girl.

Boots still slept on Temp's back, but her forehead was cooler. The medicine seemed to have quieted his dad down, too, but Gregor was still unnerved by how fragile he looked. Clearly the rats had half-starved him. He wondered what else they had done.

Ares sat hunched over in a position of such extreme sorrow that Gregor decided it was best to leave him alone. Henry's deception had nearly destroyed the bat.

No one seemed physically injured by their encounter with King Gorger's army except Aurora and himself. Gregor opened the first aid kit and fumbled around inside. If he was going to stitch up the bat, he'd better do it before he thought too much about it. He found a small pack of metal needles and chose one at random. Several spools of spinners' silk were in the kit as well. He started to ask Gox which kind he should use but stopped himself when he remembered the blue blood pouring out over her lifeless orange body. He picked out a thread that looked thin but strong.

He cleaned off Aurora's wound as well as he could and applied an ointment she told him would numb the area. Then, with great trepidation, he began to sew up the rip. He would have liked to move quickly, but it was slow, careful work mending the wing. Aurora tried to sit motionless, but kept reacting to the pain involuntarily.

"Sorry, I'm sorry," he kept saying.

"No, I am fine," she would reply. But he could tell it hurt a lot.

By the time he'd finished, he was dripping with sweat from concentrating so hard. But the wing was back in one piece. "Try that out," he said to Aurora, and she gingerly stretched her wing.

"It is well sewn, Overlander," she said. "It should hold to Regalia."

Gregor felt relieved and a little proud he had managed it.

"Now you must address your own wounds," Aurora said. "I cannot fly, anyway, until the numbness leaves my wing."

Gregor washed off his leg and put on some ointment

from a red clay pot he remembered Solovet using for wounds. His nose was another matter. He wiped off the blood, but it was still swollen twice its normal size. It was broken, most certainly, but he didn't know what doctors did for a broken nose. You couldn't really put a cast on it. He left it alone, thinking he'd probably do more harm than good trying to fix it.

Once he'd taken care of their injuries, Gregor had no clue what he should do next. He tried to assess their situation. They were lost. They had enough food for maybe one more meal. Luxa's torch had burned out, leaving only his hard hat for light. Boots was sick, his dad was incoherent, Luxa was in shock, Aurora was wounded, and Ares was in despair. That left him and Temp.

"Temp?" said Gregor. "What do you think we should do next?"

"I know not, Overlander," said Temp. "Hear you the rats, hear you?"

"When they fell, you mean?" asked Gregor. "Yeah, that was awful."

"No. Hear you the rats, hear you?" repeated Temp.

"Now?" Gregor felt a cold sickness fill his stomach. "Where?" He crawled out to the edge of the ledge on his stomach and peered out.

Rats were gathering, hundreds of them, on the banks beside the river. Several were sitting back on their haunches, their claws scraping at the chalky stone wall that flanked the waterfall. A couple tried to climb it and slid back to the ground. They began to scrape footholds in the surface. It would take time for them to scale the wall, but Gregor knew they would do it. They would find a way.

He crawled back from the ledge and wrapped his arms tightly around his knees. What were the questers going to do? Well, they would have to fly. Aurora would just have to manage if the rats climbed the wall. But fly where? The light in his hard hat couldn't last forever. Then he'd be in pitch black with a bunch of invalids. Had they gone through this whole nightmare only to end up dying in the Dead Land?

Maybe Vikus would send help. But how would he know where they were? And who knew how things were going in Regalia, anyway? Gregor and Henry had played out the last stanza of "The Prophecy of Gray." But did that mean the humans had won the war? He had no idea.

Gregor squeezed his eyes shut and pressed his palms into them. He had never felt so desolate in his whole life. He tried to console himself with the idea that "The Prophecy of Gray" had said that eight of them would live. "Well, Ripred will probably manage, but if the seven of us sitting on this ledge are going to survive, we'll need a miracle," he thought.

And that's when the miracle happened.

"Gregor?" said a puzzled voice. He wasn't really sure he'd heard it. "Gregor, is that you?"

Slowly, not willing to believe it, Gregor lifted his eyes toward the sound. His dad had weakly propped himself up onto one elbow. He was shaking from the exertion and his breath was shallow, but there was a look of recognition in his eyes. "Dad?" he said. "Dad?"

"What are you doing here, son?" said his dad, and Gregor knew his mind was clear.

He couldn't move. He should have run into his dad's arms, but he suddenly felt afraid of this stranger dressed in rat skins who was supposed to be his father. Was he really sane now? Or by the time Gregor crawled across the few feet of stone that separated them, would he again be mumbling about fish and abandoning Gregor to the darkness?

"Ge-go!" piped a little voice. "Ge-go, me out!" said Boots. Gregor turned and saw her struggling to free herself from the webbing that secured her to Temp's back. He hurried over to her and ripped away the webs. It was easier than dealing with his dad.

"Drink? Bekfest?" said Boots as he pulled her free.

Gregor smiled. If she wanted to eat, she must be better.

"Cookie?" she said hopefully.

"Okay, okay," he said. "But look, look who's here. It's Da-da," said Gregor, pointing to his father. If they went together, maybe Gregor would have the courage to face his dad.

"Da-da?" said Boots curiously. She looked at him, and a big smile spread across her face. "Da-da!" she said. She wiggled out of Gregor's grasp and ran straight into his dad's arms, knocking him flat on his back.

"Margaret?" said his dad, struggling to sit up. "Are you Margaret?"

"No, I Boots!" said the little girl, tugging at his beard.

Well, Boots's courage might only count when she could

count, but her ability to love counted all the time. Watching her, Gregor felt his distrust beginning to melt away. He had fought rats and spiders and his own worst fears to reunite with his dad. What was he doing, sitting here like he'd bought a ticket to see the event?

"Boots, huh?" said his dad. He broke into a very rusty laugh.

The laughter swept through Gregor like waves of sunshine. It was him. It really was his dad!

"Dad!" Gregor half-stumbled, half-ran to his dad and threw his arms around him.

"Oh, Gregor," said his dad with tears pouring down his face. "How's my boy? How's my little guy?"

Gregor just laughed as he felt his own tears starting.

"What are you doing here? How did you get to the Underland?" asked his dad, suddenly sounding worried.

"Same way as you, I guess," said Gregor, finding his voice. "Fell out of the laundry room with Boots. Then we came looking for you, and here you are." He patted his dad's arm to prove it was true. "Here you are."

"Where exactly is here?" asked his dad, peering around in the darkness.

Gregor snapped back to reality. "We're above a waterfall in the Dead Land. A bunch of rats are trying to scale the wall. A lot of us are hurt and we're totally lost," he said. Then he regretted it. Maybe he shouldn't have told his dad how bad it was. Maybe he couldn't handle it yet. But he saw his dad's eyes sharpen in concentration.

"How far are the rats from us now?" he asked.

Gregor slid over to the edge and looked over. He was frightened to see the rats were halfway up the wall. "Maybe fifty feet," he said.

"How about light?" asked his dad.

"Only this," said Gregor, tapping his hat. "And I don't think the batteries will last much longer." In fact, the light seemed to be dimming as he spoke.

"We've got to get back to Regalia," said his dad.

"I know, but none of us knows where it is," said Gregor helplessly.

"It's in the north of the Underland," said his dad.

Gregor nodded, but he didn't see what good that information did them. It wasn't as if they had a sunset or the North Star or moss growing on the north side of trees to guide them. They were in a big, black space.

His dad's eyes landed on Aurora's wing. "That bat, how did you sew her up?"

"A needle and thread," said Gregor, wondering if his dad's mind was beginning to wander again.

"Metal needle?" asked his dad. "Do you still have it?"

"Yeah, here," said Gregor, pulling out the pack of needles.

His dad took a needle and pulled a small stone out of his pocket. He began to rub the stone along the needle in short, quick strokes. "Get some kind of bowl. Dump out that medicine if you have to," said his dad. "And fill it with water."

Gregor quickly followed his instructions, still unsure. "So, what are we doing?"

"This rock — it's a lodestone, magnetic iron ore. There

was a pile of them back in my pit. I kept one in my pocket just in case," said his dad.

"Just in case what?" asked Gregor.

"Just in case I ever escaped. I had some pieces of metal back there, too, but nothing the right size. This needle is perfect," said his dad.

"Perfect for what?" asked Gregor.

"If I rub the needle with the lodestone, I'll magnetize it. Basically I'll turn it into a compass needle. If we can get it to float on the water without breaking the surface tension . . ." His dad gently slid the needle into the water. It floated. Then, to Gregor's amazement, the needle turned forty-five degrees to the right and held steady. "It will point north."

"It's pointing north? Just like a compass?" asked Gregor in astonishment.

"Well, it's probably off a few degrees, but it's close enough," said his dad.

Gregor grinned into the bowl of water. It was going to be okay. His dad was back.

The sound of claws digging into stone wiped the grin off his face. "Aurora," called Gregor. "Can you fly?"

"I think I must," said Aurora, clearly aware of the rats.

"Ares, if I point you toward Regalia now, can you stay on course?" asked Gregor, giving the bat a little shake.

"I can stay well enough on course if I know the direction to fly," said Ares, rousing himself.

"Mount up!" called Gregor, just as Vikus had when they'd started the quest. "Mount up, we're going home!"

Somehow everyone got loaded up. Gregor had Temp ride with Luxa, just to keep an eye on her. He slid Boots in the backpack and helped his dad onto Ares. He checked the needle in the bowl one more time and pointed Ares in the right direction. "That's north. That's the way to Regalia," he said.

Gregor was about to retrieve the bowl when he saw the first rat claw catch the top of the ledge. He leaped onto Ares's back and the bats took off, leaving the bowl and a pack of cursing rats behind.

Ares followed the tunnel that headed north, and after about an hour he called to Gregor: "I know now where we fly."

They flew straight for Regalia now, down wide, open caverns.

Everywhere there were victims of the war. Gregor saw the bodies of rats, humans, roaches, spiders, bats, and other creatures he didn't even know lived in the Underland, like mice and butterflies. No, Ripred had mentioned butterflies, but Gregor thought he had seen them in the Overland somehow. All the bodies looked the same. Very, very still.

It was almost a relief when the light on his hard hat finally gave out. He had seen enough carnage. In the darkness he lost all track of time.

Gregor could hear the horns signaling their approach long before they reached the city. He looked down vaguely and saw people waving their arms, shouting. Neither he nor Luxa responded.

Luxa was not even looking. From the moment they had

taken off, she had wrapped her arms around Aurora's neck and closed her eyes to the world. Gregor couldn't imagine what she must be feeling. He had his dad back. Boots was safe. They would go back to the Overland and his family would be together again. But Henry was Luxa's family, and he had given her over to the rats. What was there left for Luxa to feel now?

The doors were flung open at the stadium, and the city appeared below them. There was cheering and waving of flags. The palace came into view, and Ares dove for the High Hall.

They coasted in, and the exhausted bats simply landed on their bellies and slid along the floor until they stopped. Underlanders swarmed them. Somewhere in the confusion he saw Dulcet cradling Boots and hurrying from the hall with the ever-faithful Temp behind them. A couple of people laid his dad on a stretcher and whisked him away. The bats could barely protest as they were carried away, too, more in need of rest than medical attention.

Gregor resisted all attempts to be loaded on a stretcher, although he did accept a cold cloth for his nose. Someone needed to tell the story, and he didn't think it could be Luxa right now.

There she stood, pale and lost, not even noticing the whirlwind around her. Her beautiful violet eyes were vacant, and her hands hung limply at her sides. He went to stand at her side but he didn't touch her. He just let her know he was near. "Luxa, it's going to be okay," he said. He knew the words sounded hollow.

The room cleared out, and he saw Vikus hurrying toward them. The old man stopped a few feet in front of them, deep lines of concern cut into his face.

Gregor knew he had to say what had happened, but all that came out was, "Henry was working with the rats. He made some deal for the throne."

Vikus looked at Luxa and opened his arms. She stood, still frozen, staring at him as if he were a complete stranger.

"Luxa, it's your grandpa," said Gregor. It seemed like the best and most important thing to say at the moment. "It's your grandpa."

Luxa blinked. A tiny tear formed at the corner of her eye. A battle took place on her face as she tried to stop the feelings rising up inside her.

The feelings won, and to Gregor's great relief, she ran into Vikus's arms.

CHAPTER

26

It was Solovet Gregor ended up telling the story to. She appeared shortly after Vikus and, having kissed Luxa's wet cheeks, embraced Gregor. If he was not concerned about his injuries, she was. She immediately led him down to the hospital section of the palace to be treated.

While doctors cleaned and stitched his leg and tried to bring down the swelling in his nose, Gregor spilled out everything that had happened since they had parted. The journey through the rancid caves, the arrival of the spiders, Henry's attempt to kill Ripred, Boots's fever, Tick's sacrifice at the bridge, finding his dad, and the strange series of events that had fulfilled Sandwich's prophecy.

When he had finished, he felt like a balloon someone had let all the air out of. He just wanted to see his dad and Boots and then go to sleep. Solovet led him first to Boots, who was in a nursery with other sick kids. She had been bathed and changed and while she was still warm to the touch, Dulcet promised him the illness was not serious.

"We cannot cure many things still, but we can cure this. It is just a case of damp fever," she said soothingly.

Gregor smoothed back Boots's curls and went on to see his dad. His father already looked better, his face relaxed in sleep. The Underlanders had not only bathed him, but they'd groomed his hair and beard. The foul rat skins had been replaced by silken garments. They'd fed him and given him a calming medicine.

"And when he wakes, will he be okay?" asked Gregor.

"No one who spends years with the rats can expect to be unchanged," said Solovet gently. "But will his mind and body heal? I believe so."

Gregor had to be satisfied with that. He himself would never be the same after what he'd witnessed in the Underland. He had to expect some changes in his dad, too.

As he left the hospital, he heard a happy voice cry out, "Overlander!" Mareth caught him up in a big bear hug. Gregor was glad to see Mareth was alive, although he had injuries from recent battles.

"Hey, Mareth," he said. "How's it going?"

"It goes darkly, as it always goes in war. But you have brought back light to us," he said firmly.

"Oh, yeah?" said Gregor. He'd pretty much forgotten that part of the prophecy.

An Overland warrior, a son of the sun,
May bring us back light, he may bring us back none.

So he must have done it after all. Brought back light. He wasn't really sure how, but if Mareth said so, all the Underlanders must believe it.

"What light?" he asked. The images that filled his head were relentlessly dark.

"When news of King Gorger's death reached the rats, they fell into chaos. We have driven them far back into the Dead Land. Without a leader, they are in total disarray," said Mareth.

"Oh. Good," said Gregor. "I hope it lasts."

Mareth took him to his old room, the one he'd shared with Boots. He took a short bath, just to lose the smell of rotten eggs that clung to him from the dripping tunnel, and fell into bed.

When he awoke, he sensed he had slept a long time. For the first minute or two, he lay in drowsy security, not remembering. Then all that had happened flashed before his eyes, and he couldn't stay in bed any longer. He took a second bath and then ate the food that had appeared in his room while he was gone.

Gregor was about to go to the hospital when Luxa ran into his room. Her eyes were red from crying, but she seemed her old self.

"Gregor, you must come! Hurry!" she said, grabbing his arm and pulling him after her.

His first thought was that there'd been an attack on the

palace, but that was not it.

"It's Ares! They mean to banish him!" gasped Luxa as the two of them sprinted down the corridors. "He did not know, Gregor! He did not know of Henry's plot any more than I!"

"I know he didn't!" said Gregor.

They burst into a room Gregor had not yet seen. It was like a small arena. Several hundred bats and humans sat on elevated bleachers that rose up around a central stage. In the front row sat members of the Regalia council, including Vikus and Solovet. In the middle of the stage, alone and stooped, stood Ares.

When Gregor and Luxa ran onto the stage, Aurora fluttered out of the bleachers to join them.

"Stop!" yelled Gregor, trying to catch his breath. "You can't do this!" He didn't know all the ins and outs of banishment, but he did remember Luxa saying that no one survived living in the Underland alone for long. Maybe a rat like Ripred could, but he was extraordinary under any conditions.

Everyone rose to their feet at Gregor's appearance and bowed in unison. "Welcome, Warrior, and many thanks for all you have brought us," said Vikus formally. But he also gave Gregor a sad smile that felt much more personal.

"Yeah, you're welcome," said Gregor. "What are you doing to Ares?"

"We are about to vote on his fate," said Vikus. "There has been much debate about whether he was privy to Henry's plot."

"He wasn't!" said Gregor. "Of course, he wasn't! Or I wouldn't be standing here. He saved me and let Henry fall when he realized what was happening!"

"He was bonded to Henry," said a large red bat. "It is difficult to believe in his innocence."

"What of my innocence?" asked Luxa, her voice tight. "No one was nearer to Henry than myself. Will you banish me as well?"

An uncomfortable murmur ran through the room. Everyone knew how close the cousins had been, and yet Luxa had been the target of Henry's treachery.

"Even if Ares is cleared on charges of treason, there is still the issue of his breaking of the bond," said the red bat. "That is in itself a cause for banishment."

"Even when you find out you're bonded to a really evil guy?" asked Gregor. "Seems like there ought to be a special rule for that."

Several members of the council began to dig through piles of old scrolls, as if hoping to find an answer to his question. But others were clearly after blood.

"Whether he is banished for treason or bond breakage, I care not. I just want him gone. Who among us could ever trust him again?" shouted a woman.

There was an uproar in the arena. Ares seemed to hunch down even further, as if crushed by the weight of the anger against him.

Gregor didn't know what to do. He couldn't stand by and watch them throw Ares out into the Dead Land to fend for himself. But how could he change their minds?

The red bat echoed the last words Gregor had heard clearly. "Yes, who among us could ever trust him again?"

"I could!" yelled Gregor, silencing the crowd. "I trust him with my life!" And then he knew what he needed to do.

He ran to Ares and extended his hand. The bat lifted his head in puzzlement, then understood. "Oh, no, Overlander," he whispered. "I am not worthy to accept."

Gregor reached out and grabbed the claw on Ares's left wing with his right hand. You could hear a pin drop in the room as he spoke the words.

"Ares the flier, I bond to you,"

That was all he could remember of the pledge Luxa had told him, but she was right behind him, feeding him the words in a whisper.

"Our life and death are one, we two.
In dark, in flame, in war, in strife,"

And the last line came to Gregor without prompting.

"I save you as I save my life."

Some hope had come back into Ares. The warrior bonding with him was no guarantee he would escape banishment, but it was something that could not be easily ignored. Still, he hesitated.

"Say it," said Gregor softly. "Please say it back."

And Ares finally did, replacing his name with Gregor's own.

> *"Gregor the human, I bond to you,*
> *Our life and death are one, we two.*
> *In dark, in flame, in war, in strife,*
> *I save you as I save my life."*

Gregor stepped back to face the crowd. He and Ares stood before them, hand still locked to claw. Gregor spoke with a power that was entirely new to him. "I am the warrior. I am he who called. Who among you dares banish Ares, my bond?"

CHAPTER

27

There was anger and argument and a lot of talk about the law, but in the end, they couldn't banish Ares. The fact that Gregor bonded with the bat carried more weight than he had expected.

One old man still dug furiously through his scrolls until Vikus said to him, "Oh, stop rattling your skins, we clearly have no precedent for this."

Gregor turned to his new bat. "Well, I probably won't be here much longer."

"It matters not," said Ares. "While I have flight, I will be here always for you."

As soon as things settled down, Gregor made a beeline for the hospital. He braced himself before entering his dad's room, fearing he might have relapsed, but when he went in, a happy scene awaited him. His dad was sitting up in bed laughing as Boots tried to feed him cookies.

"Hey, Dad," he said with a smile.

"Oh, Gregor . . . ," said his dad, beaming at him. His dad held out his arms, and Gregor rushed into them and held on tightly. He could have stayed there forever, but Boots was tugging on them.

"No, Ge-go, Da-da eat cookie," she said.

"The nurse told her to make me eat, and she takes her job very seriously," said his father with a smile.

"You feel okay?" asked Gregor, not letting go.

"Oh, a few square meals, I'll be as good as new," said his dad. They both knew it wasn't that simple. Life would never be the same again, but they would have their life back, and they would have it together.

Gregor spent the next few hours just hanging out with his dad, Boots, and Temp, who came in to check on the princess. He wouldn't have asked his dad about his ordeal, but he seemed eager to talk. "That night, the night I fell, I couldn't sleep. I went down to the laundry room to play a little saxophone. I didn't want to wake anybody."

"We fell from there, too!" said Gregor. "Through the air duct."

"Right. The metal grate just started banging up and down out of nowhere," said his dad. "When I went to check it out, I got sucked right down here. See, they have this strange phenomenon with the air currents. . . ." And his dad went on for twenty minutes about the scientific aspects of the current. Gregor didn't know what he was talking about, but it was great just to listen to him.

"I was in Regalia for a couple of weeks and I was just going crazy missing you all. So, one night I tried to escape with a couple of flashlights and a BB gun I found in the museum. Rats got me before I made it to the Waterway," said his dad, shaking his head.

"How come they let you live?" asked Gregor.

"It wasn't me. It was the gun. After I ran out of ammo, they closed in on me. One of them asked about the gun, so I just started talking a blue streak about it. I convinced them I could make them, so they decided to keep me alive. I spent my time making weapons that I could use, but that fell apart when the rats touched them. A crossbow, a catapult, a battering ram. Lucky thing you showed up when you did, I think they were beginning to suspect I was never going to make them anything that worked twice," said his dad.

"I don't know how you stood it," said Gregor.

"I just never stopped believing I'd get home again," said his dad. A cloud came over him, and he had a lot of trouble getting the next question out. "So, how's your mom?"

"Probably not too good right now," said Gregor. "But she'll be fine once we get you back."

His dad nodded. "And you?"

Gregor didn't talk about any of the bad stuff, just the easy stuff. He told his dad about track and school and playing his saxophone at Carnegie Hall. He never mentioned spiders or rats or what he'd been through since his dad had disappeared.

They spent the afternoon playing with Boots, trying to

make each other eat and often, without any particular reason, reaching out to touch each other.

Dulcet showed up eventually and insisted Boots and his dad needed rest, so Gregor wandered off into the palace feeling happier than he had in two years, seven months, and he no longer cared how many days. He was done with the rule now. For good. Even if times got bad, he would never again deny himself the possibility that the future might be happy even if the present was painful. He would allow himself dreams.

As he was making his way back to his bed, he passed the room he'd been taken to as a prisoner the night he'd tried to escape Regalia. Vikus was sitting at the table alone, surrounded by piles of scrolls and maps. His face lit up when he saw Gregor, and he waved him into the chamber.

"Come, come, we have not yet spoken since your arrival," he said eagerly. "How does your father?"

"Better. Much better," said Gregor, sitting across from Vikus.

"And the princess?" said Vikus with a smile.

"She's good. No more fever," said Gregor.

For a minute they just sat there, not sure where to begin.

"So, Warrior . . . you leaped," said Vikus.

"Yeah, I guess I did," said Gregor, grinning. "Lucky Ares was there."

"Lucky for Ares, too," said Vikus. "Lucky for us all. Know you the rats are in retreat?"

"Mareth told me," said Gregor.

"I believe the war will soon be at an end," said Vikus.

"The rats have begun to battle one another for their throne."

"What about Ripred?" said Gregor.

"I have heard from him. He is assembling a party of rats sympathetic to his cause in the Dead Land. It will not be an easy task to take leadership of the rats. He must first convince them that peace is desirable, and that will be a long struggle. Still, he is not an easy rat to ignore," said Vikus.

"I'll say," said Gregor. "Even other rats are afraid to fight him."

"With good reason. No one can defend themselves against him," said Vikus. "Ah, that reminds me. I have something for you. Several times on the journey you made mention of your lack of a sword. The council asks me to present you with this."

Vikus reached beneath the table and brought out a long object wrapped in very thick silk. Gregor unrolled it and found a stunningly beautiful sword, studded with jewels.

"It belonged to Bartholomew of Sandwich himself. It is the wish of my people that you accept it," said Vikus.

"I can't take this," said Gregor. "I mean, it's too much, and besides, my mom won't even let me have a pocketknife." This was true. On Gregor's tenth birthday his uncle had sent him a pocketknife with about fifteen attachments, and his mom had put it away until he turned twenty-one.

"I see," said Vikus. He was watching Gregor carefully. "Perhaps if your father kept it for you, she would allow it."

"Maybe. But there's another thing . . . ," said Gregor. But he didn't know how to say the other thing, and it was the main reason he didn't want to touch the object in front of him. It had to do with Tick and Treflex and Gox; it had to do with all the creatures he'd seen lying motionless on his trip back. It even had to do with Henry and the rats. Maybe he just wasn't smart enough, maybe he just didn't understand. But it seemed to Gregor that there must have been some way to fix things so that everybody hadn't ended up dead.

"I pretended to be the warrior so I could get my dad. But I don't want to be a warrior," said Gregor. "I want to be like you."

"I have fought in many battles, Gregor," said Vikus cautiously.

"I know, but you don't go looking for them. You try to work things out every other way you can think of first. Even with the spiders. And Ripred," said Gregor. "Even when people think you're wrong, you keep trying."

"Well, then, Gregor, I know the gift I would wish to give you, but you can only find it yourself," said Vikus.

"What is it?" said Gregor.

"Hope," said Vikus. "There are times it will be very hard to find. Times when it will be much easier to choose hate instead. But if you want to find peace, you must first be able to hope it is possible."

"You don't think I can do that?" said Gregor.

"On the contrary, I have great hope that you can," said Vikus with a smile.

Gregor slid the sword back across the table to him. "Tell them I said thanks, but no thanks."

"You cannot imagine how happy I am to deliver that

message," said Vikus. "And now you must rest. You have a journey tomorrow."

"I do? Where? Not back to the Dead Land?" said Gregor, feeling a little ill.

"No. I think it is time we send you home," said Vikus.

They put a bed in his dad's room that night so that he and Boots could sleep close by. Now that he was going home, Gregor began to let thoughts of Lizzie and his grandma and, most of all, his mom come back into his head. Would they still be okay when he got back? He remembered his talk with Vikus, and tried to hope for the best.

As soon as his dad and Boots had woken, they were taken to the dock where Gregor had made his escape the first night. A group of Underlanders had assembled to see them off.

"Ares will take you to the portal above the Waterway," said Vikus. "It will be a short distance from there to your home."

Mareth pressed a handful of paper into his hand. He realized it was money. "I took it from the museum. Vikus said you may need it to travel in the Overland."

"Thanks," said Gregor. He wondered exactly where the Waterway gateway was in relation to his apartment. He guessed he'd find out soon enough.

"The way is safe now, but do not tarry. As you know, things can shift quickly in the Underland," said Solovet.

Gregor suddenly realized he would never see these people again. He was surprised by how much he would miss them. They'd been through a lot together. He hugged everybody good-bye. When he came to Luxa, he thought maybe he should just shake her hand, but he went ahead and hugged her, anyway. She actually gave him a hug back. It was a little stiff, but then, she was a queen.

"Well, so if you're ever in the Overland, drop by," said Gregor.

"Perhaps we shall see you here again someday," said Luxa.

"Oh, I don't know. My mom's probably going to ground me for the rest of my life just to keep me safe," said Gregor.

"What means this, 'ground you'?" asked Luxa.

"Never let me leave the apartment," said Gregor.

"That is not what it says in 'The Prophecy of Bane,'" said Luxa thoughtfully.

"What? What's that?" asked Gregor, feeling panic rise up in him.

"Did Vikus not tell you? It follows 'The Prophecy of Gray,'" said Luxa.

"But I'm not in it. Am I? I mean, I'm not, right? Vikus?" said Gregor.

"Ah, you must depart directly if you mean to catch the current," said Vikus, slipping the backpack with Boots onto his shoulders and leading him to Ares, who was already carrying his dad.

"What aren't you telling me? What's 'The Prophecy of Bane'?" insisted Gregor as he felt himself lifted onto Ares's back.

"Oh, that," said Vikus dismissively. "That is very vague. No one has been able to explain it for centuries. Fly you high, Gregor the Overlander." Vikus gave Ares a sign and he spread his wings.

"What is it, though? What does it say?" shouted Gregor as they rose into the air.

"Bye-bye, Temp! See you soon!" said Boots waving cheerfully.

"No, Boots, no! We're not coming back!" said Gregor.

The last thing Gregor saw as they left the palace was Vikus waving. He was not sure, but he thought he heard the old man say, "See you soon!"

Down the river he went again, but this time he was flying over the foaming water on Ares's strong back. They soon reached the beach where he'd encountered Fangor and Shed. He caught a glimpse of the blackened ground where the fire had been.

Ten minutes later, the river fed into what was either a sea or the biggest lake Gregor had ever seen. Giant waves rolled across the water's surface and crashed onto rocky beaches.

A pair of guards on bats appeared and escorted them over the water. Gregor didn't see any rats around, but who knew what else might be down here looking for a meal. He caught a glimpse of a twenty-foot spiked tail as some creature flipped it out of the waves and then dove. "Not even going to ask," he thought.

The guards held their positions as Ares began to ascend into a vast stone cone. At the base, it may have been a couple of miles in diameter. A strange misty wind seemed to be blowing them upward. "Must be the currents," thought Gregor.

Ares flew in tighter and tighter circles as they ascended. He had to close his wings to squeeze through the opening at the top.

Suddenly they were zipping through tunnels that looked familiar. They were not built of stone, but of concrete, so Gregor knew they must almost be home. The bat landed on a deserted stairway and nodded his head upward.

"I cannot go farther," said Ares. "That is your way home. Fly you high, Gregor the Overlander."

"Fly you high, Ares," said Gregor. His hand wrapped tightly around Ares's claw for a moment. Then he let go. The bat vanished in the darkness.

Gregor had to help his dad up a long flight of stairs. There was a stone slab in the ceiling at the top. When Gregor pushed it aside, a wave of fresh air hit his face. He pulled himself out and his fingers found grass. "Oh, man," he said, hurrying to help his dad out. "Oh, man, look."

"Moon," said Boots happily, pointing into the sky.

"Yes, moon, little girl. Look, Dad, it's the moon!" His dad was too winded by the climb to answer. For a few minutes they just sat in the grass, staring up at the beauty of the night sky. Gregor looked around and realized by the skyline that they were in Central Park. He could hear the traffic just beyond a row of trees. He slid the stone slab back in place and helped his dad up.

"Come on, let's grab a cab. Go see Mama, Boots?" he asked.

"Ye-es!" said Boots emphatically. "Go see Mama."

It must have been very late. Hardly anyone was out on

the streets, but a few restaurants were still open. It was just as well since they made a funny sight, all dressed in their Underland clothes.

Gregor flagged down a cab and they piled into the backseat. The driver either didn't notice or didn't care how they looked. He'd probably seen everything.

Gregor pressed his face against the window, drinking in the buildings, the cars, and the lights! All those beautiful lights! It seemed to take no time at all to reach their apartment. He paid the driver and added a huge tip.

When they came to the front door, his dad pulled out his key chain, the one Gregor had made him, from his pocket. He fanned out the keys with trembling fingers and found the right one. For once the elevator wasn't broken, and they rode up to Gregor's hall.

They opened the apartment door softly, not wanting to wake anyone. Gregor could see Lizzie asleep on the couch. From the bedroom he could hear his grandma murmuring in her sleep, so she was okay.

A light was on in the kitchen. His mother sat at the kitchen table, as still as a statue. Her hands were clasped together, and she stared fixedly at a small stain on the tablecloth. Gregor remembered seeing her that way so many nights after his dad had disappeared. He didn't know what to say. He didn't want to scare her or shock her or ever give her any more pain.

So, he stepped into the light of the kitchen and said the one thing he knew she wanted to hear most in the world.

"Hey, Mom. We're home."

ACKNOWLEDGMENTS

First, I want to thank that brilliant children's book author, James Proimos. Without his encouragement and generosity, I would never have pursued books. I owe him a great deal for introducing me to our agent, Rosemary Stimola. Editors tell me she's the best in the business, and I have no reason to doubt it. For many years before I met her, my lawyer, Jerold Couture, skillfully guided me through the brambles of the entertainment business, and for that I will always be grateful.

Special mention must be made here of Jane and Michael Collins, my parents and, as it happens, the best research team on the planet. Much love and appreciation goes to them for helping me map out life both in and out of books.

I have to single out two writer friends from a field of many for their specific contributions. An early conversation with Christopher Santos was immensely important in sending this book in its current direction. Richard Register, I confide in you so consistently and on such a variety of topics that I just have to make one global thank-you for all you do.

I'm struggling for words to express how lucky I feel that I landed Kate Egan for my editor. She is so full of talent, insight, and patience, and I can't imagine having developed this book with anyone else. Many thanks also to Liz Szabla for her expert guidance and support, and to the great team at Scholastic Press.

I wrote most of this book at other people's houses. Dixie and Charles Pryor, Alice Rinker, and Deb and Greg Evans, I'm not sure when or if I would have finished this had you not opened up your homes to me and shared your quiet spaces.

Gregor the Overlander is, first and foremost, the story of a family. I have been blessed with a large and loving one. So here's to the clans of Collins, Brady, Pryor, Rinker, Pleiman, Carmosino, Evans, Davis, and Owen for being such constants in the ever-shifting world.

And speaking of family, the greatest thanks go to my husband, Cap, and my kids, Charlie and Isabel, who bring me back light every day.